Rainbow Party

Rainbow Party

PAUL RUDITIS

Simon Pulse

New York London Toronto Sydney

This book is a work of fiction. Any references to historical events, real people, or real locales are used fictitiously. Other names, characters, places, and incidents are the product of the author's imagination, and any resemblance to actual events or locales or persons, living or dead, is entirely coincidental.

SIMON PULSE
An imprint of Simon & Schuster
1230 Avenue of the Americas, New York, NY 10020

Designed by Christopher Grassi
The text of this book was set in Trade Gothic.
Manufactured in the United States of America
Simon Pulse edition June 2005
10 9 8 7 6 5 4 3 2 1
Library of Congress Control Number 2005920707
ISBN 1-4169-0235-X

For Chip, Susan, and Lili

1:00

1:01

Gin took the slender shaft of the tube in her palm. She gave a gentle tug along the base and watched as the lipstick extended to its full length. Her eyes darted to the sides, making sure no one was watching as she tilted the ruby red tip to her lips.

"Gin, that's disgusting!" Sandy shrieked as she came around the row of lipstick displays.

Busted.

Gin quickly pulled the red lipstick away from her mouth before she had a chance to test it.

"It's not like they have testers here," Gin hissed, shooting a look at the saleslady. The woman was staring at them, probably because of Sandy's outburst.

She wouldn't be having this problem if they were shopping at ULTA or Sephora instead of a tacky kids' store like Pizzazz! This was the only place Gin could afford to buy the half dozen lipsticks she needed for the "party." The store's Teen Taboo line had a perfect selection of colors. It was convenience that had brought her there.

"I can't believe you were just going to try on that lipstick," Sandy said. "Someone else might buy that."

"How else am I supposed to know if I'm a"—Gin checked the name of the color—"Harlot?" The obvious joke was just waiting to be made, but Gin knew Sandy wouldn't go there.

"I think you're more a Candy Apple," Sandy suggested, proving the point. She held up a painfully bright color that was more suited to sports cars than body parts.

"Who gives a fuck?" Gin grabbed the lipstick from Sandy and dropped it into her yellow basket. "You can be boring red. I want something with a little more . . ."

"Pizzazz?" Sandy asked.

"Yes. That's exactly what I was going to say, Sandra Dee," Gin said.

"What?" Sandy asked. "What did I say?"

"Never mind," Gin replied. Sometimes Sandy could be so juvenile.

They were almost at the end of sophomore year. Pretty soon they'd officially be juniors . . . upperclassmen . . . upperclass*women*.

Then again, Gin's plan for the afternoon called for Sandy to become a woman just a little sooner.

"I want something wild," Gin said, grabbing another tube. "Like Electric Orange."

"Or Ginger!" Sandy said, holding a washed-out lipstick that looked more like a sunless tan gone wrong. "You know like—"

"Don't say it," Gin warned. "Ginger" was what her parents called her. She had given it up when she entered high school last year. But her parents just refused to let go.

At least they stopped calling me Ginny.

Gin dropped the Electric Orange into her basket and left the Ginger tube on the clearance table beside them. No one was going to pay full price for it, anyway.

"Check this out," Sandy said with a giggle as she held up a purple lipstick. "Jammin' Jam. Who would wear that on their lips?"

"Perry?" Gin suggested.

"Why would Perry . . . oh . . . I get it." Sandy wasn't laughing. "Is he really coming to the party?"

"That's what Hunter said," Gin blew off the question. "I'll believe it when I see it."

"Doesn't seem like his kind of thing."

"No . . . not exactly," Gin said with a smile.

"Then why did you invite him?"

"Hell if I know," Gin said. "Hunter wanted me to."

"And you can't say 'no' to Hunter."

"Oh, I can say 'no.' I just haven't found a reason to yet." Gin held out another purple lipstick. "How about Plum? The name's not exciting, but it's a decent shade."

Sandy examined the color. "That would look good on Rose," she said thoughtfully.

"Yeah . . . whatever." Gin dropped the lipstick in her basket.

"If you hate her so much, why did you ask her to come?"

"How else was I going to get Ash there?" Gin replied. "Besides, I don't *hate* her,"

"You don't *like* her either," Sandy reminded her friend.

Honestly, Gin just had no patience for the female half of Harding High's cutest couple of the sophomore class. Rose and Ash were the kind of sickeningly cute couple that made Gin want to puke. Especially when they acted all weird, doing things they thought were hilarious but were just stupid, as far as she was concerned. Gin didn't know why Rose embarrassed herself in public like that.

"Let's just say . . . I wanted to see if I could add a little spice to their relationship," Gin smirked. And by "spice," she meant conflict. Gin not-so-secretly hoped that the end of the party would also be the end of the cutest couple.

Bitter? Yes. But Gin was okay with that.

"You invited Jade, too," Sandy said. "And I *know* you hate her."

"'Hate' is such a strong word," Gin said.

Gin was smart enough to know if she had limited the party to just her girlfriends, it would be a very small one: Namely her and Sandy. It's not that the girls at school didn't like Gin. It was more like they *tolerated* her. Not that Gin wasted any energy trying to be friends.

She was much more popular with the boys. Which is the way Gin wanted it.

Sandy was the only girl who actually hung out with Gin regularly. Followed her was more like it. But Sandy was the kind of girl Gin's parents wanted to see her hanging with. And Gin liked to keep up appearances, especially where her parents were concerned. Sandy was a very good cover.

"I can't believe we're doing this," Sandy said, shaking her head.

"Shopping?" Gin asked, like she didn't know what Sandy was talking about.

This Rainbow Party thing had seemed like a good idea when Gin first heard of it. Well, actually it sounded like a gay political group, but once she found out what it really was, her interest level shot up a thousand percent. But now, with only two hours until party time, she was actually starting to get nervous too. Normally, Gin didn't "do" nervous. It was such a waste of emotion.

But so many questions kept popping up in her head.

What if no one comes?

Will I really be able to keep it a secret until it's over?

If the girl/boy ratio is uneven, how will I balance out the equation?

That last question had come to her during algebra. Instead of wondering what would happen when two trains traveling at different speeds met (most likely death and destruction, if on the same track), all Gin could think about was what would happen if six boys showed up, but she and Sandy were the only girls. Aside from the damage it would do to her reputation, it would wreak havoc with all the devious plans she had for the party.

"Okay, we've got red, orange, and purple," Gin said. "Now we just need yellow, green, and blue."

"Don't forget indigo," Sandy said as she scanned the rows of lipstick tubes.

"What are you talking about?"

"Indigo," Sandy repeated as if that explained everything. "You know: ROY G. BIV. Red, orange, yellow, green, blue, *indigo*, violet."

"That's seven lipsticks. Only six girls are coming. We don't need it."

"What if someone crashes? Or brings a friend?" Sandy asked the innocent question that was haunting Gin.

"That won't happen," she said, as if saying it out loud made it true. Gin didn't know what she would do if anyone unexpected showed up. Every person on the guest list was chosen for a specific reason. There was no room for surprises.

"It doesn't hurt to be prepared." Sandy pulled a tube out of the display.

"Thanks for the Girl Scout lesson."

"Actually, that's Boy Scouts. The Girl Scouts—"

"Fine. Add it to the pile, just in case. But you're paying for it." Gin held out her basket, and Sandy dropped the extra one inside.

Gin focused on the colors she knew they would need,

comparing Key Lime with Olive U. She put them both back, settling on the aptly named Envy.

I wonder if Jade will come, she thought.

"Check this out!" Sandy squealed, showing off a bright yellow lipstick. "It's called Banana. Get it?"

Yeah. She got it.

Gin grabbed the tube and put it with the others. Banana, Electric Orange, Plum . . . it was beginning to look like a grocery store. On the bright side . . . five down, one to go . . . and a spare just in case someone unexpected shows up.

If Subset A is greater than Subset B, then . . .

"We need to find a blue that really stands out," Gin said, checking out the rows. "Something like . . . Sapphire!" She yanked the lipstick off the display and tore off the lid. The color was bold but not overly so, with a touch of a shimmer effect.

Perfect.

"I love it," Sandy said with just the right amount of awe in her voice. It was as if Gin had shown her the Holy Grail as opposed to a mixture of synthetic dyes pressed into an obscenely phallic shape.

On the way to the register, Gin threw a tube of Harlot in with the others. The bright red lipstick was for her personal collection. She deserved a treat for pulling this whole thing together.

Gin dropped her little basket on the counter. She wondered if the saleslady had any idea what she'd be using those colors for. Girls probably didn't go around purchasing a rainbow selection of makeup at Pizzazz! every day.

Or maybe they did.

The weird part was that Gin kind of *wanted* the woman to suspect that something was going on. The best part of being up to no good is when people know you're up to no good, but can't do a thing about it.

"Have a nice day," the saleslady said as she handed Gin a small plastic bag with a big PIZZAZZ! logo emblazoned on the side.

This party is going to be off the hook, she thought. *As long as everyone shows up.*

"Should we hit the party store?" Sandy suggested. "I think a few balloons and some streamers would really look great in your living room."

Gin stopped suddenly, forcing a mother pushing a stroller to swerve to the left to avoid hitting her. "You've got to be kidding."

"What?" Sandy said as she stopped too. "Decorations."

"This isn't a balloons-and-streamers kind of event," Gin said sharply.

Sandy didn't think it was a bad idea. If you're going to have a theme party, it makes perfect sense to decorate that way. That's what she did when she had the Hello Kitty party for her last birthday.

Too bad it didn't work out the way she had hoped.

In hindsight, Hello Kitty wasn't a great theme for her first coed party. She didn't realize how much fun the boys would have with it . . . and not in a good way. They started by putting her dolls in obscene poses and went from there.

But the girls had been much worse.

They all treated Sandy like a pariah for having picked such a childish theme. The worst part was that they didn't even have the nerve to say anything to her face. They just all talked about it in loud whispers.

Boys always got a bad rap for being mean and cruel because they were so obvious about it. But nothing could match the vicious power of a girl armed with condescension and sarcasm.

Just because Gin's Rainbow Party was a different kind of party, Sandy thought, didn't mean they couldn't have some fun. It was called a *Rainbow* Party, after all. It was like the easiest theme to decorate around.

"Why can't it be a balloons-and-streamers kind of party?" Sandy asked. "I mean, first you didn't like my idea about the invitations—"

"Are you still on that?"

"It's a good idea."

"It sucked. What exactly did you want us to put on the invites?" Gin asked.

"You know . . . the usual stuff," Sandy replied. "The time . . . directions to your house . . . maybe draw some rainbows or some . . . oh . . ." Sandy's mental picture of the invitations wasn't exactly the kind of thing she wanted her mother to accidentally find. "I know . . . I know . . . 'Sandra Dee.'"

"Exactly."

Sandy was getting tired of that "Sandra Dee" nickname Gin had given her. It came from *Grease*, and Rizzo's song about Olivia Newton-John's character, Sandy, in the movie. To Gin, it was the worst possible insult. She considered immaturity the ultimate sin. And when it came to guys, Sandy's maturity was at about fourth-grade level.

Gin's stories always sounded so exciting. The things she did were almost so unbelievable that Sandy couldn't help getting caught up in them. When Gin would describe what it was like being with a boy, Sandy couldn't help but get a vicarious thrill from it. At the same time, Sandy hated to listen because all she could think about what how far *she* had never gone with anyone.

When Sandy stopped to think about the reality . . . the actual things that Gin did . . . she was almost disgusted by her. Sandy wasn't so sure that she'd ever want to be like that. She was *really* not sure she'd be ready for it by three o'clock that afternoon.

When Gin first told her she was going to throw a party, a Rainbow Party, Sandy's mind was full of Care Bears and Strawberry Shortcake. She knew it sounded odd, since Gin rarely liked childish things like that—even for their retro appeal. But Care Bears and Strawberry Shortcake stuff were sold at Hot Topic right next to Good Charlotte, Metallica, and Iron Maiden. Sandy assumed that rainbows from the 70s were the new "in" thing.

She was only partially right.

When Gin explained what a Rainbow Party was, Sandy had assumed she had heard wrong. She knew that Gin was . . . experienced . . . but this was something else. This was just plain *dirty.*

Sandy wasn't experienced in the least. She had never even kissed a boy. Well, except for Johnny Carter. But they were both six years old at the time and he had pushed her in the mud afterward, so that didn't really count. That one kiss was nothing like the deep romantic kisses she had dreamed of having. Those dreams never included . . . well . . . what Gin was planning. And now she was helping Gin prepare for it.

It was much easier to focus on balloons and streamers.

"I think I need a cookie," Sandy said as she made a detour for Mrs. Fields.

As Sandy looked over the selection of semifresh baked treats, Gin said, "You know, the Spring Fling is coming up. You want to fit into a great dress, right?"

Gin was always making those kinds of comments about Sandy's weight, which was just plain ridiculous. Gin was jealous, Sandy reminded herself. Gin was always dieting and exercising so that she could be as thin as Jade Lawrence, the hottest girl in their class. Only, Sandy couldn't imagine why anyone would want to be *that* thin.

"Do you think Jade will come?" Sandy asked, hoping to change the subject. She pointed to a chocolate macadamia cookie. It was considerably smaller than the other cookies in the case. Just because she thought Gin's comment about her weight was ridiculous didn't stop Sandy from worrying that it might be true.

"Beats me," Gin said.

"You don't sound too worried," Sandy noted, taking a bite of her cookie. Gin would never admit it, but Sandy thought she seemed a little freaked over who was coming. It was odd that she didn't care about Jade showing.

"It's a win-win situation, as far as I'm concerned," Gin said. "If Jade comes, then everyone will be talking about how cool it was that she came to my party. And if she doesn't come, then everyone will be talking about how much of a loser she was for not coming. See? Win-win."

"Oh," Sandy said. She couldn't think of anything else to say, really. It was the most illogical "logic" she had ever heard. She took a second bite from her cookie and dropped the rest in the nearest trash can.

"As long as Skye comes, we'll be fine," Gin said.

"You think she will?"

"That girl needs some variety in her life," Gin said. "So, yeah. She'll be there. Besides, Skye knows the only way she's going to keep Rod is to let him go, give him some action."

Sunny knew that Gin was only interested in Rod because he had said "no" to her. Gin was always going on about how

Rod wanted to be with her but he was just too afraid of Skye finding out. Sandy couldn't stand it when Gin talked like that. It was like she was playing a kind of game and didn't care who got hurt as long as she won.

"And you know Skye doesn't go anywhere without Vi," Gin continued. "So with Rose, that gives us five girls guaranteed to be there."

"So they're all coming?"

"Sure," Gin said, not sounding "sure" in the least, as far as Sandy could tell.

Sandy wasn't that sure herself. She couldn't imagine why Rose and Skye would come to the party. Why risk what they had? If she had a boyfriend, she wouldn't even consider it. And she certainly wouldn't let him consider it either. It didn't make any sense.

Then again, it didn't make any sense that she was going to the party either. And here she was helping plan it.

"What about the guys?"

"Do you know one guy who would even consider *not* coming?"

"Rusty's going to be there?" Sandy asked, trying not to sound too enthusiastic.

"Yeah," Gin said. "It was the only way I could get Brikowski to come."

That was the first time Sandy ever heard Gin say she was interested in Brick. Then again, Gin was usually interested in most cute guys she hadn't been with yet. It didn't really mean anything. But that wasn't the important part. *Rusty* was who Sandy wanted to come.

Sandy was glad to hear that. She knew Gin and Rusty had hooked up once, but Gin wasn't interested in him anymore. This cleared the way for Sandy. Not that this was the way to begin a relationship, but she always got so nervous when she talked to him. Maybe this would help her get over that.

Sandy's longest conversation with Rusty had been when she was covering for Gin, who had taken off with Steve Jacobs. Rusty had looked so hurt. He must have really liked Gin. Sandy had no intention of telling him that her friend didn't feel the same way. The only reason Sandy was able to talk to him for so long was because she didn't want him to find out what Gin was up to. It must have worked, because—as far as Sandy knew—Rusty never found out about Gin and Steve.

Gin was always so calm around guys. Sandy wished some of that would rub off on her. Obviously she didn't want all of Gin's habits to rub off, but a few of the useful ones might be nice.

Sandy's mind was full of Rusty when she realized they weren't heading for the exit. "Where are we going?"

"To check out dresses for the Spring Fling," Gin said, referring to the ninth- and tenth-grade equivalent of the Prom.

"I don't know if I'm going," Sandy said. "No one's asked me."

"Just wait," Gin said. "Once word gets out about this afternoon, you're going to suddenly find yourself very popular."

Sandy wished she hadn't thrown out the rest of the cookie. She wasn't sure that this was the kind of popularity she wanted. It was fine for Gin, who didn't seem to mind the reputation she had, but Sandy was different. She was very much aware of the way everyone felt about Gin. She didn't want any of that for herself.

Then again, she was also tired of always being the "good girl"; the one everyone knew would never do anything even remotely considered wrong. Gin's life seemed so much more fun . . . disgusting at times, but thrilling, too.

Sandy was ready for a bit of excitement in her life too. She was sick of being treated like she was so immature . . . like she didn't know anything about boys or sex or anything. While it was true that she didn't have any experience, she was more than ready to learn.

She was ready to say good-bye to Sandra Dee.

At least, she *thought* she was.

1:13

PLZ

don't beg

UR killing me

we'll C

ILU

DEGT

SRY

L8R

how much L8R?

EOD G2G TTFN

CYA

"I swear, I'm never going to speak good English again," Skye whispered as she closed her cell phone. She brushed a strand of her long brown hair behind her ear.

"What's up?" her best friend Vi asked softly, glancing over her shoulder toward the back of the room.

"Take a guess," Skye said. "Rod's driving me crazy."

"He couldn't wait till class was over?"

"Apparently not," Skye said, sliding her phone back into her purse.

"What did we ever do before text messaging?" Vi asked, just above a whisper.

"Write notes to each other. On paper."

"Seems positively archaic now."

"Pretty soon we'll just be wired into each other and project our thoughts back and forth," Skye said, thinking of her boyfriend three desks behind her and one row to the right. She wasn't crazy about the idea of him knowing what was on her mind at the moment.

"Just get me in a room with Christian Bale," Vi said. "I have a few thoughts I'd like to project to him."

"Dirty."

The two girls shared a secret smile.

The classroom they were in doubled as a science lab, so the desks were actually long tables with two or three people each. Skye preferred this setup to the cramped desk-chair combos in their other classes. It made conversations much easier.

Vi's other best friend, Perry, usually sat with them, but he had ditched class—probably with *his* other best friend, Hunter. Even with the extra table space, Vi slid her chair closer to Skye so they could gossip.

Skye's boyfriend, Rod, was seated in the last row. That's where he sat in every class. He did that to avoid getting called on, but Skye knew that teachers were onto that old trick. She always chose a seat in the center of any room. Far enough from the teacher so she was free to talk, but close enough that she didn't look suspicious.

"He keeps telling me he loves me," Skye finally admitted out of the blue.

"What?" Vi said a little more loudly than she should have. "That's huge news!"

And it would have been huge news, if he meant it. But Skye knew better than to believe that, especially considering why he kept saying it.

"Vi, is my lesson interrupting your conversation?" Ms. Barrett asked from the front of the classroom. "I can imagine how your topic of discussion is so much more important than mine."

"Sorry," Vi said brightly. She leaned back in her chair in silence.

Skye knew that was only good for about thirty-five seconds. Then Vi would be leaning in asking all kinds of questions about Rod's recent declarations of love. Not that Skye had any answers.

Skye did want to talk about it with her best friend. She wanted to tell her mom about it. Hell, she wanted to shout it out to the entire school. It was the first time anyone real (besides family) had said he loved her. She tried to act like she was above such silly things, but deep down she was just as mushy as the girls she usually made fun of. Like Rose. Skye totally made fun of Rose behind her back, even though she really liked her.

The thing was, Skye was pretty sure that Rod didn't really mean it when he said he loved her. It had just taken her a while to realize it. She couldn't even respond the first time the words came out of his mouth. But the second time it happened, she realized the truth. It was just like when her little sister would say, "I love you," or even "I hate you," depending on the situation. Rod wanted something. And Skye knew what it was.

At first, she was angry. How dare he say those words when he didn't mean them? Then, she realized that she had never said them back. And, truthfully, she wasn't nearly as upset as she should have been. That was when the truth hit her harder than Rod's first surprise announcement of love.

She didn't love him. She liked him. But she didn't love him.

She *wanted* to love him. She'd never admit it to anyone, but she wanted to have what Rose and Ash had: the kind of teen relationship that they wrote about in movies starring Lindsay Lohan (but not Hilary Duff). But there were no over-produced bubblegum pop songs playing in the background of her romantic scenes with Rod.

"So, tell," Vi said after thirty-seven seconds. (Skye checked the time on her watch.)

"Nothing *to* tell," Skye replied.

"Oh my God! You have got to be kidding! When? Where? How?"

"Why?"

"Skye! You're *killing* me," Vi said. She was taking this far more seriously than she should have been. She was also taking it far more seriously than Skye was.

"When . . . last week. Where and how . . . you don't want to know. Let's just say we weren't exactly dressed at the time."

"Did you tell him you love him back?"

"Why would I do that?" Skye knew she was being snippy for no reason. Well, no . . . there *was* a reason. The reason was she was frustrated because she *couldn't* tell him she loved him back. Not to mention the fact that she suspected he didn't honestly mean what he was saying.

"Why *wouldn't* you do that?" Vi said. "Rod is perfect for you. Why don't you—"

"Hold on," Skye said. "I want to hear this."

Skye really didn't care what Barrett was talking about up at the chalkboard. She just needed a break. Vi was asking very logical questions, but Skye knew that logic had nothing to do with her relationship with Rod. And since she didn't have any answers, she'd rather not talk about it at all. While it was true that ignoring problems didn't make them go away, not dealing with them made them much easier to deal with. *If that makes any sense.*

Besides, the class discussion was on STDs. That was a topic that was kind of useful to her, as opposed to other stupid things she was supposed to be learning in school. It didn't hurt to be informed. Although Ms. Barrett wasn't really saying anything that Skye could relate to.

It was all so clinical. Sure, it was good to know these things, but she'd rather talk about what it was really like to have sex. When she and Rod were together, she wasn't thinking of bacteria and viruses and repercussions. She was worried about if she was doing it right, how to tell him what she wanted . . . why he always seemed to finish while she was just getting started. Those were the real questions she had. Then, maybe if she had some of those answers could she think about the other things.

If anyone could have answered her questions about sex, it would have been Ms. Barrett. She was the only adult Skye knew who could deal with the "health issues" and still teach reality. The class had been much more helpful last week. Skye was actually learning about herself in terms she could understand and even relate to. But that was before the school brought down the hammer on Ms. Barrett in the form of Abstinence Only Education.

Thanks a bunch, Allison Monroe.

Skye knew it wasn't really Allison's fault. But everyone was blaming her, so it was just easier to go with the flow.

The problem had started innocently enough last week, when Ms. Barrett had harmlessly asked if everyone knew what masturbation was. The ensuing class discussion was actually interesting and informative. For the first time Skye even stopped worrying about the fact that she often preferred spending more time "with herself" instead of fooling around with Rod. Apparently, this was perfectly natural. Unfortunately, the discussion set off a chain reaction of events.

Allison was president and founding member of the Celibacy Club. At their last meeting, Allison had talked about what Barrett had taught that week. As the story goes, Allison was just trying to start another discussion. It wasn't like she was ratting Barrett out or anything. But Mrs. Steiner, the faculty adviser, went ballistic over what Barrett had said, and it all kind of blew up from there.

And now everyone was blaming Allison and the Celibacy Club.

Of course, if this hadn't happened, people would find some other way to make fun of the Celibacy Club. Never let it be said that the kids at Harding High didn't know how to prepare a proper smear campaign, especially when presented with such an easy target.

On the surface, the Celibacy Club was one of the more contradictory groups at school. It was the kind of club where kids—mostly girls—would walk past the classroom a couple times before they went inside for the meeting. As if they were embarrassed to join a club whose members proudly declared their intention to wait until marriage.

Skye certainly had moments in her life when she wished she could rewind time and reclaim her virgin status. The loss of it had happened so quickly, she wasn't sure she was even remembering what had happened correctly. Everyone always talked about knowing when the moment was right. Well, at the time, Skye thought she knew it was the right time. It certainly seemed right. But honestly, she wasn't really thinking with her brain in the moment. Things hadn't happened at all the way they were supposed to . . . the way she had planned it.

Now, looking at Allison—the only one actually taking notes in class—Skye wished it was all just a game and she could have a do-over.

Wouldn't that be nice? To go back and do it again with someone who really *loves me.* She actually respected Allison a little for being able to run that kind of a support group knowing how much of a target it made her.

Not that she'd ever tell Allison that.

Skye's cell phone made her bag vibrate, bringing her back to reality. Skye knew it was Rod texting her again. Instead of going into the bag, she shot him a glare over her shoulder.

He was staring directly at her. His eyes were *begging* her to pick up the phone.

"So, *are* we going to this thing at Gin's?" Vi asked as Ms. Barrett moved the discussion from syphilis to gonorrhea.

"Haven't decided yet," Skye replied casually. The

"casual" part was an act. She had been freaking out about the decision ever since Gin had told her and Rod about it. But she didn't want Vi to know that. There were appearances to maintain, after all. If Skye was supposed to be the "experienced" friend, how would it look if Vi really knew how she felt?

"But feel free to do what you want," Skye added.

"I'm not going if you're not going," Vi replied.

Skye felt the same way. Skye probably wouldn't go if Vi decided to stay home. This wasn't the kind of thing you went to without some moral support . . . or immoral support, as the case may be.

Then again, it was kind of weird to think of her boyfriend and her best friend. . . .

"Does Rod want to go?" Vi asked.

"What do you think he keeps bugging me about?" Skye asked. "Although, he *has* been incredibly attentive this week."

"You mean more than usual?"

"He's been text messaging me and constantly leaving cute little notes in my locker. That kind of stuff," Skye said. She really did like the attention, even if there was an ulterior motive attached.

"Wow. He must really care about you."

"Or he must *really* want to go to the party," Skye said.

Vi was always trying to make Rod into some romantic leading man. She kept talking about how good he was to

Skye and how well he treated her. Skye didn't argue. He *was* a great guy. She wouldn't be going out with him if he weren't. But they didn't have one of those historic love affairs that everyone dreams of, that Skye truly dreamed about. It was more like they were just really, really good friends . . . with benefits.

It didn't help that both Rod *and* Vi were waiting for Skye to make her decision about the party. It was like they couldn't decide on their own. Well honestly, Rod couldn't go without her. At least she hoped that he wouldn't.

It was bad enough trying to figure out whether she wanted to go. Skye didn't need the extra pressure of deciding for anyone else. So instead of deciding, she did what she usually did in these situations: She put it off.

There was a brief pause in the conversation while Barrett showed a truly disgusting picture. Since Skye hadn't been listening, she didn't know what the photo was showing, but she knew she didn't want it to happen to her.

Maybe I should be paying more attention.

Vi tried to focus on the party. And ignore the fact that she just found out that Rod had admitted he loved Skye. It didn't really help that Skye was acting like she didn't even care. If a guy—*any* guy—had told Vi he loved her, she would take out a page in the *Harding Herald.* A full-page ad in the school paper with **HE LOVES ME** in big bold letters . . . with hearts, even.

No boy had ever told Vi that he loved her. And the way things were going, it didn't look like anyone would be saying it to her anytime soon.

Considering the pictures Ms. Barrett was holding up, maybe that wasn't such a bad thing.

"Why is she showing that to us?" Vi whispered to Skye.

"Probably to scare us out of having sex . . . ever," Skye replied.

Vi had had enough. She couldn't look at the ugly STD photos anymore. She played with her charm bracelet instead. Whenever she was bored in class, she usually found herself spinning the silver heart-within-a-heart, the biggest charm on her bracelet.

It was actually her mom's bracelet. Her dad had bought it as a gift when they were dating in high school. Her parents had been together ever since. They still acted all sweet with each other in ways that would probably make most kids die of embarrassment. But Vi wasn't most kids. She hoped to find someone she could feel half as much love toward to spend her life with.

Actually, she just hoped to find someone. The "life" part could come later.

Once again she thought of Skye and Rod. Her best friend had a boy, ready and willing to admit his love for her, and it was like she didn't even care. What was more annoying was how close Vi had come to being the one Rod had fallen for.

She and Skye had been in the auditorium on the first day of school freshman year, waiting to be put into their homeroom groups. They were busy catching up since they hadn't seen each other all summer, because Vi was with her grandparents in New York.

It was crowded and loud, but Vi really loved the energy of the place. It was a new school and a new start.

That's when she saw Rod's golden blond hair up in the sunlight as he came into the auditorium from outside. She knew guys didn't like to be called "beautiful," but that was the only word that had come to mind when she saw him.

Vi could have sworn he had been coming over to her, but once the introductions took place and he made the expected comment about a pair of girls named Skye and Vi being best friends, Skye's natural exuberance took over, leaving Vi's shy silence in the dust.

Skye and Rod started hooking up almost immediately. Well, they weren't really dating at first. But it wasn't until the following summer that their relationship got *serious.* And Vi wasn't even around for this. When sophomore year started, not only were Skye and Rod officially "together," they had even done things that, to this day, Vi didn't want to know about.

But Skye told her anyway.

"Look at Allison," Skye whispered.

Vi looked over and saw Allison furiously taking notes. No doubt she was coming up with discussion points for the next Celibacy Club meeting.

Vi had a real problem with the Celibacy Club. Everyone in the club talked all about never having sex until they were married. As far as Vi was concerned, that was just plain nuts. There was nothing wrong with making love so long as both you and the guy *were* in love.

That was one of the reasons it bothered her so much that Skye was having sex with a guy she just admitted she didn't love. Not that it was any of Vi's business. Of course, Skye kept trying to make it Vi's business. Which was especially annoying because when Skye would brag about being with Rod she didn't really care about what Vi had to say about it. It seemed like Skye just wanted to say things out loud but didn't want to deal with them.

If Skye ever did ask her opinion, Vi had a speech all ready about how Skye should just appreciate what she had, since other people would kill for a guy like Rod. He may not be perfect, but really, who is? He was only in high school. All it would take is some work to make him perfect. And he was well worth the investment.

That's exactly what Vi would tell her friend. If Skye ever asked.

Skye's purse emitted another buzzing sound. It was probably Rod again.

Poor guy.

"Aren't you going to get that?" Vi asked.

"So we can play another round of Please-No-Please-No?" Skye said. "I don't think so."

Vi continued to look at the buzzing purse, aware that Skye was staring at her.

Eventually, Skye pushed the purse over to her friend. "You deal with him."

"Are you sure?"

"What do I care?"

Vi took what she felt was the appropriate amount of time to pause before diving into the purse and pulling out the phone.

-Y NOT?

Is what she saw on the screen.

Vi checked to make sure Barrett wasn't looking in her direction, then waved the phone to show Rod she was going to respond.

HEY, she started.

sup
workin' on her
THX
FWIW I'll B there
GR8
really?
lukin fwd 2 it
me 2
keep me posted
will do TTFN.
BOL

Vi scrolled back through the messages to the one that said he was "Looking forward to it." She wondered what the "it" was referring to. Did he mean that he was looking forward to her being at the party or that he was just looking forward to the party itself?

Vi was still not sure how she felt about this afternoon. Her mind kept going back and forth on the issue. A year ago she wouldn't have even considered going to such a thing. But now part of her was excited by the idea, especially after Rod had told her he was looking forward to it.

It wasn't like she had the kind of experience that Skye had. She was certainly nowhere near Gin's level. But what girl in their school was?

Vi was still a virgin. And she was in no huge rush to change that. She was waiting for the right guy to come along before she was going to give that up.

She did have *some* experience, though. Brad, for instance. He lived in New York; Vi met him over the summer. She fooled around with him a few times. They never had actual sex, though. She knew she didn't love him and had no intention of going all the way.

He kept asking her to, though. He kept *begging* her, in fact. But she wouldn't. That was when he stopped talking to her. That had really hurt. She knew Brad didn't love her, but she thought he was interested in her for a little more than just action.

She knew she never should have gone as far as she had,

but she couldn't help herself at the time. Not coincidentally, the first time she had actually gone down on him (or "kissed him down there," as Brad put it), it had been the day after Skye called to tell Vi about her first time with Rod.

Even though she kind of regretted the things she had done with him, she was so glad she hadn't actually had sex with him. Some mistakes she could forgive herself for, but that was one mistake that she wasn't about to let herself make.

"Well?" Skye asked.

"I'm going to go to the party. It might be interesting to check things out," Vi replied without even thinking. Once the words were out of her mouth, she instantly regretted the decision. There was nothing *interesting* about the party. There was probably nothing *fun*, either. If anything, it seemed more like a story someone like Hunter would make up to brag about to his friends.

But for some reason, Vi really, really wanted to go. Especially since Skye was considering going. That made it safer.

"What did Rod say that made up your mind?" Skye asked, curious.

"Just that he really wants to go," Vi said. "I'm thinking if one boy wants to go that badly, imagine how the others feel. Could be fun."

"True," Skye replied.

Vi also thought it might be a good way to get in some

practice for when she was with a guy she loved. Brad wasn't really much help in letting her figure things out on her own. He was always in such a rush to finish before his parents got home. But the guy she eventually fell in love with might appreciate the fact that she knew what she was doing when it came to some things. Especially if he was experienced.

She wasn't necessarily looking for someone who was also having his first time. It might be nice to be with a guy who knew what he was doing. Someone who could guide her. Someone who loved her, and someone she loved.

Someone like . . . Rod.

"Rod, what's going on?" Steve Jacobs whispered from beside him. Since they were all the way in the back of the class, he didn't really have to speak so softly. As far as Rod was concerned, he didn't have to speak at all. Just because he and Steve were on JV football together, it didn't mean they were friends.

"What are you talking about?" Rod asked as he put down his phone. He had been holding it pretty much since class began, trying to figure out some way to convince Skye they should go to Gin's.

"Is it about the party?"

Rod froze.

"What?" Rod asked.

"That Rainbow Party thing," Steve said. "You're going, aren't you?"

"What the hell are you talking about?" Rod asked. "Do I look like somebody who likes rainbow crap?"

"No man, it's a sex party," Steve said. "Some chick is throwing it, but I don't know who."

That's a relief.

And, technically, it's not a sex *party. It's just oral.*

Rod was pretty sure that Gin and Steve had hooked up a few times. At least, that's what Steve said. If she hadn't invited Steve, then she obviously didn't want him there. That was fine, as far as Rod was concerned.

Rod knew there were several ways to play this. He just had to pick the right one. "Wait a minute," he started. "A *girl* at this school is throwing a sex party? You're out of your mind."

"No man, it's true. I heard—"

"And what makes you think I'd go to such a loser party?" he continued. "I don't need some party to get action. I got all I can handle."

That part he did say softly because he didn't want Skye to hear him. She didn't like it when he bragged about being with her. She especially didn't like it when he exaggerated. Sure, they were having sex, but it wasn't like they were doing it all the time. In fact, she only let him have full-on sex with her on special occasions. That is, occasions *she* determined as "special." He never really understood why. If she was willing to do some things with him, then why not everything?

The funny part was that some other girls were willing to do everything with him all the time. But with them, he only went so far. It was one thing to fool around on Skye, but it was not his style to totally cheat on her.

"You mean you really haven't heard?" Steve asked.

"I'm trying to listen to Barrett," Rod replied, putting an end to the discussion.

He really didn't need any more guys at the party getting in his way.

If he was *allowed* to go.

Rod wondered when things with Skye had gotten to the point where he had to ask her permission to do anything. It was like he had to clear his schedule with her every day just to make sure they were spending enough time together. Not that he totally minded. He liked spending time with Skye. And not just when they were fooling around. But lately she had a way of making everything seem like a chore. It was much more fun when things just happened spontaneously. Somehow they had gotten serious a lot faster than he had intended.

One day they were just having fun, and the next they were a *couple.* But it wasn't like he didn't know how it happened.

Sex.

It changed everything.

Sure, it was great to have a girlfriend he could have fun with, but he wanted more. That was one of the reasons he was so excited about this party. There would be plenty of girls there. If only there weren't other guys, too.

It was always possible that some of the guys would bail . . . but not Hunter. He'd definitely be there cutting in on the action.

Hunter could get any girl he wanted. Rod probably could too, in fact. He noticed more than a few stares in the hallways. The problem was that Rod didn't have the luxury of sampling at Harding High. There were probably any number of girls he could get. But he wouldn't do that to Skye.

Besides, he knew how the grapevine worked. If he ever hooked up with another girl from school, word would get back to Skye before he even got his pants back on.

Oh sure, he got a little action on the side every now and then. But he went outside of school grounds to find those girls. And those hookups were never as fun as they could be. Even though they came with the added benefit of knowing he was doing something he shouldn't be doing, Rod had found there was a fine line between guilt and good times.

Rod tried to put sex out of his mind. He knew that old stat about guys thinking about sex every thirteen seconds . . . or nine seconds . . . or three seconds. Rod thought about it every second. He was a slave to his penis.

Barrett's lesson was so boring he couldn't manage to focus on that, either. Even those disgusting pictures she had shown a minute ago did nothing to soothe his hormones.

Usually, he wouldn't be so bored in Barrett's class, especially when the topic was sex. Barrett was one of the hottest teachers in school, as well as the star of several of Rod's favorite fantasies. But that had changed last week.

Thanks a lot, Allison.

Rod knew that he hadn't helped the situation any. People weren't just talking about the Celibacy Club's reaction to Barrett's lesson. They were also blabbing about what he had said. When Barrett had asked if the class knew what masturbation was, he couldn't help but blurt out his reply:

A waste of time when you've got a girlfriend who'll go down on you.

He didn't know why he had said it. No . . . that's not true at all. It was Steve. The idiot wouldn't shut up about all the girls he had been with. Rod knew most of it was lies, but he still felt like he had to show Steve up for some dumb-ass reason.

Skye was still making him pay for the unfortunate outburst. And now he wasn't even sure if he'd be allowed to go to this thing at Gin's. There it was again . . . being *allowed* to go. Life was so much easier when he didn't have to ask his girlfriend's permission to do things. But he wasn't willing to think about letting her go.

Of course, now he couldn't even enjoy sex ed. The principal must have really laid in hard on Barrett, because she was going out of her way to steer clear of "questionable material."

". . . in addition to frequent and often burning urination, a persistent sore throat is also a possible, though more rare, sign of gonorrhea," Ms. Barrett continued her lecture. Few people were listening to any of it. He could tell by the number of heads resting on desks. "Other symptoms include . . ."

Oh, screw this, Rod thought as the hand shot up in the air and he threw a *watch this* smile to Steve.

"Yes, Rodney," Barrett said. She was using his full name defensively, obviously knowing where the discussion was about to go.

Rodney. His parents should have just given him a tattoo at birth that read, PLEASE, KICK THE CRAP OUT OF ME. At least everyone called him "Rod." That sounded almost porn star by comparison.

"I'm confused," Rod said as he pulled down his hand. "How can you get a sore throat from having sex? How would your throat be involved?"

Barrett shot a very obvious look toward Allison as most of the students' heads rose from their desks. "I think, Rodney, that you can use your imagination on that one. There are different forms of sexual intimacy."

Rod's hand shot up again. "I'm sorry," he said without being called on. "But I follow a strict belief of abstinence only." This got laughs from several of his classmates, and not just the boys.

Skye, however, was not laughing. He felt bad about that, but not bad enough to stop.

"I guess that means you were just making things up with

that comment from last week," Barrett interrupted, pushing the envelope. "It's good to know that you're still a pure, virtuous young man."

This evoked several "wooos" from the class.

Once the noise settled down, Rod continued his attack. "I'm confused about these different forms of sexual intimacy. Can you explain them to us? In graphic detail, preferably."

"Yes, I probably could," Ms. Barrett replied. "However, I've been instructed to veer our class discussions away from . . . sensitive subject matter."

Even from his seat in the back of the class, Rod could see that Allison was blushing and sliding down in her chair.

"But how is protecting us from gonorrhea a 'sensitive matter'?" he continued. "I would think that, in these dangerous times, it would be best to be informed about such things."

"And you would be," Ms. Barrett replied, "if I didn't totally rely on my meager paycheck to keep a roof over my head and food on my table. Suffice it to say there is one particular sexual variation that could result in the disease coming in contact with the mouth and throat."

"Oh, you mean blowjobs!" Rod said as if he suddenly understood.

Allison spun around and shot him a look begging him to stop. Rod knew this was only making Allison feel worse about the whole situation being blown out of proportion. But he didn't really care. It was the most fun he'd had all day.

"Yes, Rodney, I am referring to oral sex," Ms. Barrett said. "And again I must remind you that abstinence is the . . . only . . . school-recommended way to protect against these diseases."

"But blowjobs aren't really sex."

"Rodney"—she continued to use his given name more in this class period than she had used it all year—"I do not intend to get into a discussion on the definitions of sexual intercourse. Suffice it to say, *oral sex* is an intimate act."

"Well, it's not like us guys have to worry about getting gonorrhea that way, right?"

"It is entirely possible for boys to contract the disease from girls as well," the teacher insisted. "So long as the girl has an attentive boyfriend who is just as interested in filling her needs as he is in filling his own."

"I'm not sure I know exactly what you mean," Rod said with a smile.

"No, Rodney," Ms. Barrett replied, matching him smile for smile. "I don't imagine that *you* would."

The entire class burst into laughter. Rod knew that he had lost the battle and it was time to shut up.

1:28

Hunter's heavy breathing was the only sound in the bathroom stall. He couldn't help it, considering what had just happened. It was a good thing whoever had just come into the boys' room hadn't stumbled in ten seconds earlier.

Hunter wasn't really worried they would be caught. The book bags were strategically placed so if anyone counted legs under the door they'd only come up with two. Knowing that if he looked down he'd start laughing, Hunter focused on the words on the bathroom stall instead:

FOR A GOOD TIME DON'T CALL ALLISON MONROE.

While totally old-school, truer words had never been written in a bathroom.

Hunter wished he had written it himself. The idea of Allison being a "good time" gave him a laugh, and so few things at Harding High did that. He also took it as a challenge. Imagine how his reputation would grow if he ever managed to get in the pants of the head of the Celibacy Club.

As far as Hunter was concerned, the Celibacy Club was a total waste for a babe like Allison. It was also bullshit. He knew the truth. Girls wanted it the same as boys. All that crap about waiting for marriage and being in love was just for show. There was one thing they wanted, and he couldn't blame them at all.

Finally, the urinal flushed.

The phantom pisser didn't bother to wash his hands and was out of the bathroom moments later. Once he heard the door close, Hunter cracked up. "Wow! That was excellent," he said when he could finally speak again.

"Thank you," his best friend, Perry, said as he stood.

"Man, I owe you one."

"Actually, you owe me forty-seven."

"Dude. You've been counting?"

Perry's eyes went wide. "No. I was making a joke. How pathetic do you think I am?"

"Relax. Take a breath."

Perry did as instructed. He was good at taking directions.

Hunter burst out laughing again.

"Are you going to pull up your pants?" Perry asked.

"I gotta take a piss."

"Oh," Perry said, but didn't move.

"You planning on watching?"

"Sorry." Perry picked up his backpack and moved toward the door.

Hunter shifted to let his friend pass. They had to squeeze together for Perry to get by. As he made his way out, Perry's hand brushed across Hunter's bare ass. Hunter wondered if it was an accident, but pushed the thought out of his head. *Nah. He isn't that way.*

Once Perry was out of the stall, Hunter slid the lock in place without really knowing why. It wasn't like Perry was going to see anything he wasn't already intimately familiar with. But it still felt weird. Just like the idea that he'd grabbed Hunter's ass on purpose. Or the possibility that Perry had counted the times they had done what they just did.

It wasn't the first time Perry had made an indirect reference to expecting Hunter to reciprocate. He just wasn't into it the way Perry was. Sometimes Hunter worried that he was using his friend, but Perry seemed to be enjoying himself. And what good would it be to stop them both from enjoying the pleasure it brought?

Hunter justified his actions—or lack of action—by getting Perry invited to Gin's. "This Rainbow thing is going to be bangin'," he said as he waited for his bladder to start emptying. Even his twisted imagination was impressed by the images it was conjuring. "I always knew Gin was kinky, but this is perverse. Gotta give the girl props for coming up with something so ingenious."

"She's a real party planner," Perry said.

"And Gin is the perfect one to pull this off. I mean that girl can do things you'd never imagine."

Hunter closed his eyes for a moment, picturing Gin in front of him. She was always so eager to please. But she was nothing compared to Perry's talent.

"You still haven't told me if you're comin' or not," he said as his eyes popped back open. "Of course you're comin'. Who am I kiddin'? You'd be crazy not to."

It was about time Perry got some action of his own for a change. He never made a move on any of the girls at Harding. There was no reason he couldn't have as much fun as Hunter. Perry had a great sense of humor and was always surrounded by girls. He was kind of good looking, too, for a guy. Just a little on the skinny side.

Hunter had so many discards around that Perry should have made out like a bandit. With all the sex he could steal.

Gin had said she didn't want Perry to come, but Hunter had gone so far as to tell her that if Perry didn't go, *he* wouldn't either. Gin was all over herself—and Hunter—convincing him that the party wouldn't be the same without him.

Hunter went through all that trouble for his friend, and Perry hardly even acted like he appreciated it.

"You want a mint?" Perry asked through the stall door.

"Later," Hunter replied as nature finally started to take its course. "You never said anything about the party. . . . But your mouth *was* kind of full at the time."

"Ha. Ha."

"Well?"

"I'm thinking about it."

"What's to think about?"

"Gee. I don't know. It's not like this thing happens every day."

"You can say that again."

"I mean, where did Gin ever get the idea in the first place? She's not usually this . . . creative on her own."

"Beats me. I think she saw it on TV or something."

"Obviously I need to watch more TV," Perry said.

Once again Hunter heard the bathroom door open. Since nothing was going on this time, he figured Perry would just keep talking, but the sudden silence told Hunter something was up.

"Hey faggot," a voice that probably belonged to Tom Lynch said.

Perry chose not to respond, which Hunter considered a mistake. Ignoring assholes like Tom never made them go away. It just made them intensify the attack. He tried to hurry up and finish what he was doing so he could join his friend, but there was only so much he could do to force his bladder to empty.

"Hey, faggot, Tom's talking to you," said the voice belonging to Tom's partner in intimidation, Jake Browning.

"You hangin' out in bathrooms nowadays?" Tom asked. "Just waiting for guys to come along?"

"Yeah," Jake echoed in typical dumb-sidekick fashion. "*Come* along."

Hunter pulled up his pants, flushed the toilet, and slammed the stall door open for effect. "Problem?"

"Aw, Hunter, we were just wondering why your little friend here was hanging out in bathrooms," Tom said with a noticeable shift in tone. He was suddenly much less threatening.

"Looks like he was waiting for me," Hunter said as he walked over to wash his hands. Perry used the distraction to move away from his tormentors, hoping to fade into the background. "I think the better question is what were you two coming here to do?"

"What are you saying?" Jake asked.

"Two guys. Alone in a bathroom when they should be in class. Sounds like a party to me," Hunter said, fully aware that he was implying exactly what he and Perry had been doing. But Tom and Jake would never make that connection.

"That's sick," Tom replied. "We're just killing time."

Hunter turned off the water. "Kill it somewhere else."

The two losers stared blankly for a moment. It wasn't often that sophomores spoke to juniors that way, but Hunter wasn't your average sophomore.

"Whatever," Tom finally said as he turned and made for the door.

"Yeah. Whatever," Jake echoed as he quickly followed.

Hunter checked his watch. He left biology over ten minutes ago. It was probably one of the longest bathroom breaks in history, but he was in no rush to get back to class. Mrs. Archer had probably forgotten he had even left the room. She was one of the more oblivious teachers in the school.

"Thanks," Perry said softly.

"Don't let those assholes get to you," Hunter said. "You're no fag."

"I know."

"Ain't nothing wrong with helping a guy out."

"Yeah, right," Perry said. "Nothing wrong with that."

Nothing wrong at all, Perry thought. But there *was* something wrong. At least as far as Perry was concerned. What he was doing was more than just "helping out." He was actually enjoying it. All forty-seven times. Yeah, he was counting too. And he could remember most of the forty-seven times . . . vividly.

But he also wanted more.

It wasn't like that made him gay. He had never kissed Hunter. Okay, there was that one time he moved in to kiss him, but Hunter pulled away. Since neither of them ever said anything about it, Perry was fine with acting like it never happened.

Perry had been "helping Hunter out" since the eighth grade. Between sleepovers and playing in Hunter's pool they had seen each other in various states of undress many times since they were kids. This particular time, it had started out innocently enough with a game of "I'll show you mine if you show me yours." Perry hadn't seen Hunter naked in a couple years and had gotten curious. Considering how his own body was changing, he was wondering if his friend's was too.

And it was.

Hunter had already been reaping the rewards of years of playing soccer. His chest was developing, and his arms were getting larger. They weren't the only things that had grown either. Hunter's pretty-boy looks had only sharpened in the two years since Perry had last seen him this up-close.

That's when their relationship changed. It started with comparing, and quickly moved on to other forms of mutual exploration. Then, once Hunter suggested that Perry put his mouth "down there," the mutual aspect of their friendship had come to an end.

Forty-seven times later, Perry was still waiting for his friend to reciprocate with that mythical "one" that Hunter owed him.

Hunter took a cigarette from his backpack and lit it without bothering to offer Perry one. Aside from the fact that Perry thought it was a disgusting habit, they also weren't supposed to smoke in the bathrooms. They weren't supposed to give blowjobs in the bathrooms either, but some rules Perry couldn't help breaking.

As Hunter raised the cigarette to his lips and inhaled, Perry wished he could be that cigarette. For Hunter to take hold of him. To feel the smooth texture of Hunter's lips as they wrapped around . . .

Then he realized how stupid he was being and changed the subject.

Sort of.

"What's the deal with this party again?" Perry asked. "I don't get the whole 'Rainbow' thing."

"Look, it's simple. Each girl puts on a different color lipstick, and the guys all drop their pants. Then the girls go down the line giving each guy head. When they're done, the guys have a rainbow of colors ringing round their dicks. Sweet."

"Ah, the rainbow erection," Perry said. "And why *are* there so many songs about rainbows?"

"What?"

"Never mind," Perry said. "But that's the part I don't get. The rainbow left behind. I mean, I'm no expert—"

"I beg to differ."

"Thanks. But wouldn't it just be a gray mess? I mean if the girls are doing it right, wouldn't the colors all blend together?"

Hunter stared blankly for a moment. It lasted long enough for Perry to wonder what Hunter was smoking. Perry sniffed the stale bathroom air, but the smoky scent was distinctly nicotine, not marijuana.

"Hunter?"

"A half dozen girls are about to go down on you and you're worried about the color aspect. Who gives a fuck if your dick looks *black* afterwards?"

"I think that might be something to worry about," Perry said. "But hey, I'm the one ditching the lesson on STDs, so what do I know?"

"You're really focusing on the wrong part, Periwinkle."

"Don't call me that," Perry said halfheartedly.

Periwinkle was the nickname Hunter had come up with for him way back in kindergarten when he realized the similarity between Perry's name and the light blue Crayola crayon. It didn't take long for Perry's dad to point out that Periwinkle wasn't the proper nickname for *his* son, so it immediately came to an end—in public, at least. Hunter still used it every now and then when it was just the two of them.

Perry acted like he hated it, but he actually loved the fact that Hunter had a secret name for him. He loved all the secrets he and Hunter shared.

"I'm just saying, maybe the rumors are true," Hunter added.

Perry opened his mouth, but nothing came out.

He knew that Hunter didn't mean what he was saying, because if Perry *was* gay, what would that mean about Hunter? But Hunter certainly wasn't above using the idea to pressure Perry into doing something that he didn't want to do. And it wasn't like the idea of a room full of half-naked guys didn't hold its appeal. Perry just wished the girls didn't have to be there.

Then, for the millionth time, he wondered what *that* meant about him.

"Let me have that mint now," Hunter said as he dropped his cigarette and crushed it on the floor. He rarely finished an entire cigarette. It was his way of trying to convince Perry that he didn't really smoke as much as he did.

Hunter was full of it on so many levels.

Perry handed him an Altoid from the tin in his backpack. He knew it was a ridiculous cliché found in romance novels, but Perry felt a charge as their fingers touched when he passed the mint. When Hunter smiled at him, Perry's face lit up in return.

Hunter could do no wrong in Perry's eyes, which accounted for how he could get away with so much. But there was another side of Hunter that needed to make sure he never hurt Perry or did anything to make Perry look down on him.

That was the worst part. If Hunter had just treated him like shit, Perry would be out of there in a second. But just when Perry had had enough, Hunter would do something to remind him of why they were friends in the first place. Then the game would begin again.

Perry must have had a hurt expression on his face, because Hunter's usual sexy smile faltered for a moment.

"Hey man, I was fucking with you," Hunter said as he gave his friend a gentle punch in the chest.

"Ouch."

"You've got to be kidding," Hunter said. "You really are a pussy."

"No it's not that. I just . . . um . . ."

"What?"

"At the mall last night . . ."

"You didn't!"

"Well . . ."

"Let me see! Let me see!"

Perry got that exciting feeling in his stomach that he usually felt when he knew he had done something that would impress Hunter. He checked the door to make sure no one was coming, then untucked his shirt. He slowly lifted the material, making sure the moment lasted as long as possible. It was almost like he was unveiling a piece of art, and his body was the work in question.

He could see the glint of silver as the bottom of his shirt rose above his right nipple.

"Shit, man. That is so cool! Where'd you get it?"

"Pizzazz!"

"They do nipples there? Right in the store? In front of everyone?"

"I doubt they do girls."

"Why didn't you tell me?"

Because this is the reaction I wanted to get.

The silver hoop hanging from his nipple looked even better than he had expected, though it was still sore from the piercing. But the pain and inconvenience were worth it for the look of excited admiration in Hunter's green eyes.

"Does it hurt?" Hunter asked as he reached out and played with the ring, carelessly rubbing Perry's nipple in the process.

"Not at all," Perry lied.

He was enjoying the intense sensation of pleasure mixed with pain.

1:29

Charlie Brikowski rubbed his hand back and forth quickly over the length of wood. It was rough, hard, and knobby, with splinters that the sandpaper was useless against no matter how hard he stroked. After five minutes of polishing he finally gave up and dropped it in the trash bin beside the table.

His best friend, Rusty, shook his head sadly. "You're just no good with wood, Brick."

"Funny," Brick replied.

With a last name like Brikowski, it figured that would be what everyone called him. Brick wasn't too bad on its own, but someone was always using it in the phrase "dumb as a . . ." While it was true that Brick wasn't exactly a genius, he wasn't an idiot, either. He just felt that way when he couldn't even make a crappy picture frame.

He might as well just give up and take the *F* in woodworking now.

Rusty was already putting together his *second* picture frame of the hour.

Show-off.

Actually, Brick knew that Rusty wasn't really showing off. Rusty was just trying to use the limited skills he had to get Jade Lawrence's attention. *He's gonna need a much bigger picture frame for that.* As far as Brick was concerned, Jade was way out of Rusty's league. Though Rusty had tons of experience when it came to girls, he was usually a putz around them. And while his idiotic charm could work on some girls, it would never work on Jade.

Then again, what the hell do I know?

Brick brought another piece of wood over to the miter saw. He turned it on and carefully went about making another cut.

Given the option, he would rather have taken home ec, but he knew he'd never hear the end of it. No matter how queer-eyed for the straight guy the world was becoming, boys at Harding High did not take home ec as an elective. Brick wasn't one of those insecure jocks who had to prove how manly he was. He just didn't need to give any of the guys another reason to give him any shit.

A month ago, Brick had made the mistake of mentioning that he was a virgin in the locker room after basketball practice. Brick was certain that he had not been the only one in the room at the time. In fact, he was pretty sure that the guys who *hadn't* seen any action were in the majority. The school grapevine was pretty up-to-date on who was doing who as well as what, where, and when.

The difference was that Brick was the only one who *admitted* that he was a virgin.

That was the equivalent of declaring it hunting season and naming himself the only target. The jokes were still flying in rapid-fire progression. Brick wasn't the only nickname he'd had lately.

Since that day, Rusty had made it his personal mission to find a girl to help get Brick over his "problem."

Brick was only fifteen, and somehow this was a "problem." Rusty treated him like he was years behind schedule. Like there was an actual schedule for these things. If there was, it was hard to imagine in what universe fifteen was considered a late bloomer. But he was the one stupid enough to admit he had never been with a girl at all. And he hadn't heard the end of it.

Like it was any of their damn business anyway.

"That's better," Rusty said over Brick's shoulder. It annoyed the hell out of Brick that Rusty treated him like a kid brother; always condescending in every situation except on the basketball court. Just because Rusty had experience in one particular area didn't make him all mature and wiser.

No matter how much of a "mission" Rusty was on, Brick wasn't in any rush to have sex. Not that he was waiting for some perfect moment, with the perfect girl. He was just afraid of coming off like an idiot. The guys always sounded so smooth when they talked about sex. Not Rusty so much, but apparently that didn't stop him from getting some.

It was like every other guy had been born automatically knowing what to do. Brick's limited experience came from watching those movies on "Skinamax" in the middle of the night.

So far, Brick had been able to put Rusty off when he suggested someone for him. No matter how lame the excuse, Rusty usually bought it. But Brick knew he wouldn't be able to get away with that much longer.

The easiest excuse was that he wasn't interested in the girls Rusty would pick out. It wasn't like the guy spent any time on it anyway. He'd usually just go around the lunchroom pointing to whatever girl walked by. Rusty once pointed at one of the lunch ladies when he wasn't paying attention. Lunch ladies aside, Rusty simply had no idea what Brick was interested in.

Not that Brick really knew either. He just knew that he hadn't found the right girl. Yet all the pressure his so-called friends were putting on him didn't help. When Rusty had brought up Gin's party, Brick knew he couldn't stall anymore. He was going to have to "put up or shut up," as Rusty so eloquently put it.

Brick didn't understand why his sex life—or lack thereof—was public property, anyway. Of course, he never said that. Instead he just said that he'd go to the party. He had finally run out of excuses.

At least Brick would finally put some of the jokes to rest this afternoon. He might still technically be a virgin when they were done, but none of the guys would ever be able to call him inexperienced again. They'd finally move on to some other victim and leave him alone.

He still wasn't sure why nobody considered blowjobs "sex," but he wasn't going to argue the point. Experience was experience, and he'd take it any way he could get it. Even if he didn't really think he was ready for it.

So instead of going home to play Halo 2, Brick was going to Gin's, where he was finally going to give in and—

"Fuck!" Brick yelled.

His right hand released the handle of the miter saw, which shut down the blade. Blood poured from his left hand, staining the wood and the metal on the saw.

"What happened?" Mr. Stokes hurried across the room, obviously recognizing the sound of a potential lawsuit.

"Nothing," Brick said quickly, hiding his hand. It was one thing to be a klutz when trying to put together a simple picture frame. It was another to cut off your finger while doing it.

Everyone stopped working. The room went dead silent, but he could swear that he already heard the stories of his idiocy spreading down the halls.

"Let me see the hand," Mr. Stokes insisted.

Brick reluctantly held his hand out. Now that he actually

saw the damage, he revised his earlier estimate. Blood was not so much *pouring* from his hand as it was *trickling.* In fact, the trickle had pretty much stopped. He had just opened up a little nick on his finger. The stain on his wood was just a drop.

"You scared the hell out of me, boy," Mr. Stokes said. "For nothing more than a cut. Go wash it up and put on a Band-Aid. You'll live."

"Good job, Brick," someone muttered.

Well, at least they'll take a break from the virgin jokes for a while.

Brick's face went as red as his nickname as he walked to the sink. The room remained silent. Everyone was still watching him like they were expecting him to do something else. He'd probably never live the story down either. Losing a finger during woodworking would have carried some element of respect. Or at the very least, pity. But *acting* like you lost a finger when it was just a little cut would make the story truly pathetic.

Brick held his finger under the cold water, wishing he *had* done more damage. A real injury would have gotten him out of class, at the very least.

But a real serious injury, like actually losing the finger—*that* would have gotten him sympathy. A trip to the hospital meant that he could probably have hung out in the waiting room all afternoon . . . instead of going to Gin's party.

That would have been a good excuse.

1:35

"Guess what it is," Rose said as she held out a small box wrapped in shiny gold paper.

Ash shoved the posters he was holding under his arm. The last thing he had expected while they were putting up the announcements for the Spring Fling was to get a gift from his girlfriend. Considering her gifts usually came at unexpected intervals, he didn't know why he was surprised.

And it always started with "Guess what it is."

He hated this game. Not because he didn't love getting gifts from Rose, but because the first thing that always jumped to his mind was, *I should have gotten her something too.*

The problem was that Ash never knew how to find that "perfect gift." Rose had such crazy taste. Just one look at her showed that. How many other girls could pull off dressing like she lived in the fifties, with beige Capri pants, a pink checked shirt, and her hair tied in a scarf as if she were going out for an afternoon riding in a convertible?

It didn't help that she acted like she absolutely *loved* everything he gave her. No matter if it was the gold (plated) necklace, or the mermaid fishing lure that came free with the purchase of the rod he had gotten his dad for his birthday. She reacted exactly the same way to each gift. Ash found it hard to believe she was just as excited about jewelry as she was fishing supplies, no matter how much she loved collecting mermaids.

"Guess," she insisted as she placed the box in Ash's hand.

"A new car?" he asked, picking at the paper.

"That would have to be one tiny car."

"The keys," he said. "I bet the car's in the parking lot. Although if it's a MINI-Cooper, it could probably fit in the box. Actually, you could probably fit two of those cars in here." He rattled the box for effect.

"Ashley Plummer," Rose said, giving him a playful slap on the arm. "I don't know why I call you my boyfriend."

"Probably because if you called me your girlfriend, people would talk," he replied. "Scratch that. People talk no matter what we call each other."

"Then I think from now on I shall call you George."

"George?" he asked. "As in Washington?"

"No."

"Jetson?"

"No."

"Of the Jungle."

"That's it!"

"Hmm, I suddenly feel the need to crash into a tree," he said.

"Might be a problem finding one around here," Rose said as she looked up and down the long hall.

"Then I guess I'll have to fake it," Ash said as he ran across the hall and slammed himself into a locker.

"Ouch," he said. He felt that one in his toes.

"Oh, George," Rose said as she ran to his side. "That was . . . really dumb."

"Yeah," he replied. "I think I'll go back to being Ash."

"That's my little Pokémon trainer," Rose said as she mussed his hair.

He could smell the rose water perfume she wore. The scent stayed with him even when she wasn't around.

It was great having a girlfriend he could be stupid with. He knew it probably annoyed everyone else, and that the cuteness level was off the charts, but he didn't care. When he was around Rose, he didn't give a damn what other people thought.

No wonder he was in love with her.

Whoa! Where did that *come from?*

"Are you okay?" Rose asked. "Got the wind knocked out of you?"

"You could say that."

She could *really* say that. That must have been one powerful crash into the locker for him to come up with the fact that he loved her.

And this wasn't that stupid "I love you so much" crap that people were always tossing around. He had said that to her a bunch of times since they started dating over a year and a half ago. Every time he said it, he felt like he had meant it. But this was different.

This time, he finally knew it for real. He didn't just love her. He was *in love* with her. He was totally, one hundred percent, absolutely in love.

So crazy in love.

Uh-oh, uh-oh, uh-oh, oh no no.

"You still haven't opened your gift," Rose said.

Ash looked down at the gift in his hand. Before his locker run he had gotten the paper off the box, but he hadn't opened it yet. He was having difficulty moving at the moment, though. His entire body—muscles, bones, joints—locked up, except for a slight tremble under the skin.

Major life realizations can do that to you.

"Just building suspense," he said.

Ash wanted nothing more than to tell Rose what he had just realized. But standing in the middle of an empty hallway at Harding High was not a place for admissions of love, particularly not when Rose was part of the equation. This was a story she'd be telling their kids.

Kids? Where the hell did that come from?

Rose was always talking about a future together, but Ash had never given it serious thought. They were only fifteen! He was just hoping they'd be together through the Spring Fling, which would then get them through summer, into next year and maybe to the Junior Prom together. The Senior Prom was too far ahead to even think about.

And now he's thinking of kids?

Rose was looking up at him with anticipation. It would be so easy to put the gift away without opening it and tell her he loved her. But he knew it wouldn't go over so well. This was neither the time nor the place. No . . . when he finally told her, it would have to be perfect. Candles a must. Romantic music, definitely. Maybe something jazzy from the forties. Rose liked that old-fashioned stuff.

It would be the perfect moment.

But it would have to wait.

In the meantime, Ash opened his gift. It was a key chain that looked like a small pack of Marlboros. He didn't smoke, but his name *was* Ash after all.

"Do you like it?"

"I love it," he said, instead of I love *you.*

"Maybe we'll get the car keys for it next time."

Ash leaned in and placed his hand on the back of her head. He gently pulled her forward and kissed her.

He wasn't usually one for PDAs at school, but at the moment, he didn't care. He wanted anyone who was looking to see how deeply he felt for her. Besides, the halls were empty. Well, except for the NTA down at the corner waiting for some poor student without a hall pass. But everyone knew that her eyes were so bad, she'd never be able to see what Ash and Rose were up to.

She didn't even say anything when he had slammed into the locker.

"Wow," Rose said as they pulled apart. "Maybe I should have gotten those car keys."

"We've got to get these posters up," he said, trying to occupy his mind with something other than *Iloveherlloveherlloveherlloveher.* The rainbow-colored posters were scattered all over the floor, having been dropped during the kiss.

They bent together and picked up the posters. By the time they were finished a pair of long—rather exposed and extremely skinny—legs had joined them. Ash looked up the length of the legs and past the barely there skirt to see Jade Lawrence, sophomore class president, standing over them.

"Hey guys," Jade said. "Hanging posters, I see."

"Spring Fling," Ash replied as he got up. His eyes were looking all over the hall, except in Jade's direction. He was trying his best not to stare at her skimpy outfit. Jade didn't normally dress like that.

Nobody normally dressed like that in school and got away with it.

"You're taking your roll as chairperson way too seriously,

Rose," Jade said. "You could have pawned that off to someone on the committee."

"Then I would have had to sit through bio instead of hanging out with my boyfriend," Rose said with a smile as she grabbed on to Ash's arm.

"Always thinking," Jade replied.

Ash looked at Rose and Jade together. They made an interesting pair. Jade was every guy's definition of perfect, and it was hard not to notice considering the outfit she almost wasn't wearing. For someone so popular, no one really knew much about her.

She never dated anyone at their high school, probably preferring college guys instead. Rumors were always swirling about just how far she had gone with those college guys.

Rose was almost the opposite. She was certainly attractive, but in a different way. She was usually just a step out of sync with popular trends, but managed to pull it off in a way that made her unique, not an outsider. Amazingly, she knew just about every one of the over three hundred students in the sophomore class and was friendly with most of them.

She certainly wasn't perfect. She was *real.* And that, more than anything, was the reason Ash was *in love* with her.

There's that crazy phrase again.

"You couldn't have approved this," Jade said as she looked over one of the posters. It had a picture of Glinda the Good Witch from *The Wizard of Oz.*

"Rose was voted down," Ash said, hoping to head off

the conversation he had already been through several times.

It didn't work.

"I wanted the theme to be Harajuku Girls," Rose quickly added. "We'd do the entire gym up in Japanese inspired decor. Then we could all dress up in crazy outfits . . . like Gwen Stefani. Even give out awards for the most fashionably insane. But do you think the students at this school would ever do something so crazy? Nope. Spring Fling is a tradition. No costumes. Only dresses and suits."

"Which leads us to this year's theme," Ash said, looking at the garish poster.

"Over the Rainbow," they said in unison.

"Could you just die?" Rose asked. "Talk about *boring.* 'Over the Rainbow' is so nineteen nineties."

"Speaking of which," Jade said, taking a moment to make sure there was no one in earshot.

Ash did the same and only saw the lone NTA, whose hearing was only slightly better than her sight.

"You're not going to Gin's party, are you?" Jade continued. It was a simple question, but for the second time in the past five minutes, Ash's entire body froze. Being majorly caught off guard can do that too.

"Yes," Rose answered so quickly that she even surprised herself. It was more shocking that she had said "yes" since she and Ash hadn't even talked about it. Well, that's not entirely correct. They had talked *around* it. They had talked within the general subject area of it. But they never actually talked *about* it.

Technically, they had been avoiding it more than anything else.

"Really? I never would have guessed you'd go."

"It sounded . . . interesting," Rose said. "We're always looking to try new things."

"Curious," Jade said, and paused for a moment. "Well, I'm off to the principal's office. I think I'm in trouble for something, believe it or not."

"I doubt that," Rose replied, and meant it.

Jade never got in trouble for anything. She never actually did anything to get in trouble for. Jade was always working on some kind of cause, whether it was food drives, or social events, or student protests. If Jade headed up the committee, students would line up to join. Sometimes just watching Jade made Rose tired.

They used to be best friends and would do everything together. That was before Jade's dad died three years ago. That was when Jade changed. It didn't happen overnight, but she slowly started getting more involved in whatever she could. She pulled away from her friends at the same time. When her mom remarried, Jade pretty much severed most of her ties with her middle school life. By the time she hit high school, she had been reinvented as the cool loner.

Friendly with everyone, but friends with no one.

Not that the change was entirely for the worse. It's just

that now she was always up to something. Her dad had been one of those cool parents who thought everyone's goal in life should be to change the world. Jade took that to heart. When she wasn't organizing committees, she was secretly scheming to make things happen, whether it was convincing their English teacher to let her read *Gossip Girl* for a book report or getting the principal to cease and desist with the random locker search policy.

Jade usually got what she wanted.

"What do you think *that* meant?" Rose asked once Jade was out of earshot. "When she said she never guessed we'd go to the party. Was she insulting us?"

"I doubt it."

Rose wasn't sure. Even though they weren't as close as they used to be, Jade was one of the few people who knew the truth about her relationship with Ash. It wasn't anything that Rose had told her. Jade just seemed to know everything about everybody. And she did it without participating in the Harding High grapevine.

"We're going to the party?" Ash asked cautiously.

Rose moved to a nearby bulletin board. "I'm sorry. I don't know why I said we were. It's just . . ."

"Jade has a way of . . ."

"Exactly." She took the case of pushpins out of her pocket while Ash held up a poster. "It's okay, right? You *do* want to go?"

"Of course . . . as long as *you* want to."

"Sure," she said as she carefully placed a pin in each of the four corners of the poster. It wasn't totally straight, but she wasn't exactly focused on that right now. "Everyone just assumes we've been doing it. Imagine how much they'll talk if we don't go. I can just hear Gin spreading rumors about us. I hate how this place is such a rumor mill."

"You know I don't do that, right?" Ash said. "I don't go around making up stories."

"I know," Rose said, and she meant it too. She had no doubt that she could trust Ash.

The thing about dating exclusively for almost two years was that everyone just *assumed* they had done it. Rose was smart enough to know that the boys would get on Ash's case if they knew the truth. That could lead to all kinds of pressure for both of them. So she told him he could let the guys think what they wanted as long as he didn't encourage it.

Sure, Ash had protested at first. He didn't want her getting that kind of reputation. He kept saying that he would wait. That it didn't matter. But she worried that eventually the pressure would get to him and he'd either push her too hard or go somewhere else. It was a dumb fear, but she couldn't help it.

Besides, it wasn't that bad to think that her reputation was that she had shared with her boyfriend the greatest gift they could give each other. She wasn't stupid enough to think that was how the rumor was spreading, but as long as she looked at it that way, it didn't really matter what anyone else thought.

And yet she had been quick to answer when Jade had asked about the party.

As they walked the mostly empty halls, Rose wondered why she let herself get into this mess. She knew it had a lot to do with Gin, but not entirely. Rose *let* Gin's argument persuade her, even though it was totally lame.

But it's not really *sex,* Gin had said. *It's just oral. And you're not even cheating on each other. He'll be right there the whole time.*

Sure, in the history of humankind there had been dumber arguments, but Rose was hard-pressed to come up with any.

To go from protecting her virginity to participating in an . . . oral sex party just made no sense. She had spent so much time worrying about Ash giving in to pressure that she never even thought about how she'd handle it. Apparently . . . not well.

"We've only got five more posters," Ash said, breaking the silence as they climbed the gray concrete stairs to the second floor. "Does that mean we have to go back to biology when we're done? Because I was hoping we'd be able to stretch this out till the end of the day. We could probably just go hang out in the student council office. No one should be there now, and it wouldn't be like we were ditching. We do have a note to get out of class. . . ."

Ash went from utter silence to rambling, but Rose hardly heard a word he was saying. She had other things on her mind. Mostly she was wondering what was on *his* mind.

". . . could probably do some work there too, so it's not like we're skipping out on . . ."

Sure, he said he was fine with going to the party. Why wouldn't he be? He was going to . . . well, she didn't want to think about what he was going to do. And she *really* didn't want to think about what she was going to do.

". . . maybe we should go back to class. . . ."

And maybe Gin was right and oral sex wasn't really sex. It didn't *seem* as intimate. But Rose had never gone even that far with her boyfriend. She wasn't sure that she was ready to, especially in a room full of people. And she knew she didn't want to do it with any other guys. But Ash had been terrific at waiting for her, and maybe he deserved this one . . . reward.

". . . but if we stall with these last five . . ."

"Here we are!" Rose said way too loudly for the empty hall as they reached a bulletin board. The second-floor NTA shot them a look because she was neither as deaf nor as blind as the one downstairs. Rose lowered her voice as she pulled out the box of pushpins. "Let's get this one up. When we're done we can hang out in the student council office."

"Okay," Ash said. He stopped babbling.

Rose looked at her watch. Gin's party was only a little over an hour away.

It was going to be a very long hour.

1:53

"Sorry to keep you waiting," Principal Hogan said as he showed Jade into his office.

"That's okay." Jade took one of the two guest chairs. She had been in the principal's office many times for her work on various school functions. This was the first time she was there for a disciplinary problem. Not that she considered her wardrobe choice a "disciplinary problem."

"Now . . . what are we going to do with you?" Principal Hogan asked as he sat behind his desk.

"You don't like what I'm wearing?" Jade asked, cutting to the chase.

"It's a bit . . . revealing."

"It is, isn't it?" Jade said with a coy smile. She was wearing a tan, cropped, long-sleeved tee that hugged her breasts and barely covered any part of her stomach, along with a green plaid skirt hiked just at the point any other girl would be showing her goods to everyone. Jade had practiced keeping the skirt from rising any higher than she wanted it to go.

"You have to know that it's not appropriate for school."

"It's no worse than what Fergie wears in her videos."

"The Duchess of York?"

"Black Eyed Peas."

"Oh," he said, as if he had any idea what she was talking about. "I hate to use a cliché, but if everyone was jumping off a bridge would you jump too?"

"It depends," Jade said. "Are they filming the jump for a reality show with a million-dollar prize? If they are, I could probably get my stepdad to drive me there."

Principal Hogan let out a heavy—exaggerated—sigh. "When you dressed this morning, you must have known that what you chose to wear was in conflict with the dress code."

"Is it?" Jade asked, honestly. "If you ask me, the school dress code is a little unclear on the subject."

Principal Hogan lifted a sheet of paper off his desk. He knew Jade well enough to be prepared before she even walked into the room. "'Skirt hems must be no higher than mid-thigh.'"

"But what is mid-thigh, really?" Jade asked. "This is high school. We're all still growing. Mid-thigh one week might be something entirely different the next. How are we to know when an ill-timed growth spurt can change the appropriateness of an outfit?"

"Somehow I think you were roughly the same height when you got dressed this morning as you are at this moment."

"And what about the shirt?" Jade moved the conversation forward. "It's long-sleeved. Covers my shoulders and arms and everything."

"Not *everything.*"

"My midriff is a tad bare," Jade acknowledged. "But I think I'm totally within the new rules on that one."

"You know we changed that language to accommodate emerging popular styles," Principal Hogan reminded her. "We could have kept the rule of 'no bare midriffs at all,' but we relaxed the restriction at the request of the students."

"So we are now allowed to have bare stomachs," Jade insisted, cutting him off.

"'While maintaining proper decorum,'" Principal Hogan reminded her of the complete rule.

"But who determines proper decorum?" Jade asked. "See. This is where we get into trouble."

"No Jade, this is where *you* get into trouble," Principal Hogan said. "You're a very bright girl. You knew that your outfit was inappropriate for school. And yet you wore it, anyway. It's as if you were daring a teacher to send you to my office."

"And it only took all day for someone to do it," Jade said. "Why is it that no other teacher in the entire school sent me here? Apparently my outfit was perfectly fine until Mr. Stokes saw me in last period."

"Enforcing the dress code is something I will be taking up with the faculty during our next in-service day," he said. "Again."

"But if the faculty doesn't understand the code, how are the students expected to?"

"Is that what this is about, Jade?"

"I swear it was an honest mistake," Jade said. "I woke up this morning and saw it was a beautiful sunny day. Even you have to admit that it's unseasonably warm for May first."

Principal Hogan relented and gave the slightest nod. It was considerably warmer than usual. At least, it was *outside.* The heat hadn't managed to warm the building yet, and it was rather chilly inside the cold cinderblock walls. Jade had spent most of the day freezing in her cropped top and short skirt.

"I guess I got carried away," Jade said with a smile. "I'd be happy to go home and change, but by the time I got back, school will already be out. If only a teacher had said something about my clothes earlier."

"I could give you detention."

"Now what kind of message would that send?" Jade asked, knowing she had won the battle. "According to the rules, if it's a first offense, the student is to be sent home to change. And I've never been called in for this before. I've never been called to your office for *any* infraction before."

"True." He was already relenting.

Jade went in for the kill. "And I'm sure my mom would

be very upset to learn I was made an example of, just because no other teacher in the school had a problem with my outfit earlier in the day."

"Now, there's no need to bring your mother into this," Principal Hogan said. He was notoriously afraid of upsetting parents.

"She's picking me up today," Jade said, checking her watch. "In fact, she's probably already here. I could just run out and get her."

"That's okay," he said. "It is almost the end of the day, isn't it?"

"Pretty much."

"And why should you be punished because my staff took all day to enforce the rules?"

"My thoughts exactly."

The principal stood. "But I expect Monday you will be dressed more appropriately? No matter how nice the weather is?"

"I wouldn't think of pushing things after today . . . sir," Jade threw in the "sir" to bring him totally to her side.

It worked.

"Then we'll let you go this time," Principal Hogan said as he escorted Jade to the door. "But remember, you are one of the class leaders. You need to be more aware of the image you project."

"Oh I am, Mr. Hogan," Jade said. "Should I go back to class now?"

The principal checked his watch. "By the time you get back to shop, the final bell will have rung."

"Probably."

"And you say your mother is waiting?"

"Definitely."

"You might as well go meet her."

"Thank you, Mr. Hogan," Jade said as she moved out the door. "I'll tell my mom you said hi."

"Yes. Do that," he replied.

Jade quickly made her way through the outer-office before Hogan realized what had happened. Not only did she get out of the principal's office with no punishment, she was even getting to go home early. She could have easily gone back to the woodworking shop with time to spare, but there really wasn't time to do anything, so what would have been the point?

Jade made a mental note that she'd have to do her picture frame tonight. Stokes had thought he was being a hardass for kicking her out of class and then telling her she'd have to make up the project on her own time. Jade had no problem with that. She would just do it in her father's workshop in the garage.

Before Jade's dad died, he had told her how important it was for a girl to know how to use her hands to build things. *No child of mine is going to need to find a man to change a light bulb,* he would say. Her sister, Jenny, was always whining about it, but Jade loved to work with her hands. Besides, being in the workshop made her feel closer to her dad.

As soon as she was out of the principal's office, Jade went straight for her locker and threw on a jacket. She was thrilled to finally be a little warmer. As she slammed the door shut, she saw Hunter and Perry coming toward her.

"Hey guys," Jade said. "Doesn't anyone stay in class anymore?"

"You know," Hunter said. "Bathroom."

"Didn't I see you walking to the bathroom like a half hour ago?"

"Would you believe I got lost?"

"Good thing Perry came along to show you the way," Jade said. "Or I suspect you'd find your way into the girls' shower."

"Then we'd never see him again," Perry said.

"Well, some of us would," Jade said, and smiled.

"What are you doing wandering the halls before the end of the day?" Hunter asked as he leaned casually against the row of lockers. There was an oddly shaped dent in one of them.

"Leaving," Jade explained. "Going to the mall."

"We are too," Hunter said smoothly.

"We are?" Perry said.

Hunter ignored his friend. "Maybe we'll see you there."

"Maybe."

"Or later?"

Jade paused, trying to figure out what he meant. The grin on his face indicated that there was some secret meaning involved, but damned if she could figure it out. "Sure. Later," she finally said.

"See you then," Hunter leered.

"Bye," Perry added with no leering at all.

Jade continued down the hall, still wondering what she had just agreed to. Since she didn't really mean it, she didn't waste too much time worrying.

Jade pushed the doors open and stepped into the warm afternoon. It felt good on her bare legs, which, as Hogan had mentioned, *were* rather exposed. The weather had very little to do with her chosen attire. The dumb school dress code was useless and poorly enforced. It also targeted the girls more than the boys. After four girls had been sent home in one day last week, Jade decided to do something about it.

She was planning to be voted junior year president based on her platform to abolish the dress code altogether. Imagine the things she'd accomplish by senior year.

Jade easily found her mom's Explorer and hopped inside

"Hi, Jackie," Jade said. Her mom did not like to be called "Mom."

"Hi, dear."

"You know, I could have just met you at the mall," Jade said as she buckled her seat belt. "It's only a couple blocks away."

"I like picking you up," Jackie said. "Besides, now we get to spend more time together."

"Uh-huh," Jade mumbled noncommittally. She pulled

her Palm Pilot out of her bag and checked the afternoon schedule. Between shopping with Jackie, calling her grandfather to wish him a happy birthday, finishing the group project for history (that she was the only one working on), *and* putting in at least one hour of charitable work at the animal shelter (it looked good on the colleges apps) she'd have plenty of time to do the picture frame . . . and anything else that may come up.

2:00

2:05

"Hey, Mom, we just got here," Gin said into the phone. Her mom liked her to check in as soon as she was home. Most kids would be all bitter, but Gin didn't mind at all. It was a very useful call to make.

"'We'?" her mom asked. She had that distracted tone she usually had over the phone. That meant she was reading something while she was talking.

"Sandy came over. I invited her for dinner. Hope it's okay."

"As long as it's okay with her mom, it's fine with me."

"Mrs. Fisher's totally cool with it," Gin said. "Sandy already asked. I'm thinking Chinese."

"I don't know," her mom replied. "Eating out is getting pricey."

"Yeah. I know. But just think of all the cooking you won't have to do."

"I don't mind cooking."

You might not, but Dad and I do.

"But I'm in the mood for Chinese," Gin said. Her mom tried really hard when it came to cooking, but nothing ever came out the way she intended. As a result, dinner at their house was usually served out of boxes made of cardboard or Styrofoam. "Besides, there's nothing in the fridge except Slim-Fast and some vegetables . . . unless you were planning on stopping at the supermarket on the way home."

"Crap," her mom said. Gin wasn't sure if her response had to do with the fact that they were out of food or if she just read something that she didn't like. "I have a meeting with Grace this afternoon. I am *not* going to be in the mood to go shopping afterward."

"You want me to call in the regular order later?"

She heard mumbling on the line. Her mom had just covered the receiver to talk to somebody. Gin waited patiently.

"Look honey," her mom said. "I've got to go. I'll call your dad later and arrange dinner."

"Bye," Gin said as her mom hung up the phone. She turned to Sandy and held out her hand. "Let me see."

Sandy handed over the carrot she had been holding.

"Mom's not coming home early today," Gin said as she examined the carrot. "I bought us a few minutes while she picks up dinner. She'll probably make it home around the same time Dad does. We're totally in the clear."

"That's good," Sandy said. It didn't sound like she meant it, though.

Gin handed the carrot back to Sandy. "See, this is a problem . . . these teeth marks. Boys don't really like it when you do this to them. You have to cover your teeth with your lips."

"Got it," Sandy said, checking out the carrot. "What should I do with this?"

"Eat it. Throw it out. I don't care," Gin replied.

Sandy looked at the carrot for a moment, then dropped it in the garbage. Gin couldn't really blame her.

"We'll start you off with Rusty," Gin said. Not only was he good for a beginner, but Gin wanted to see the reaction when she mentioned his name. It was as expected.

Gin could see Sandy's body actually tense up when she said his name. Sandy had never told Gin that she had a crush on Rusty, but it was incredibly obvious. Anytime Rusty was around, or even when Gin mentioned him, Sandy got all girly. Well, she was *always* girly, but when she was thinking of Rusty, it reached epic proportions.

"Are you sure we should be doing this?" Sandy asked. "It seems . . . dangerous."

"You and Rose must be the most innocent girls on the planet. It's not like we're having sex," Gin replied. "There's hardly any risk."

"I meant your parents. What if they come home early?"

"Oh . . . Dad's in court. Then he'll have to go back to the office. He won't be home until *way* later tonight."

"And your mom? You're sure she won't come home early?"

"Positive. Her meeting should take all afternoon."

"What if it doesn't?" Sandy asked.

"Then we've got the garage to warn us," Gin explained. "You can hear it open from every room on the first floor. We've got an average of two minutes to get everyone out the front door before Mom gets into the house."

"But if we're in the middle of—"

"I've done it before," Gin explained. "Hunter had his pants on and he was out the door before Mom even reached the kitchen."

There was really nothing to worry about. Gin had it planned perfectly, and everything was falling into place. She had the lipsticks and she was pretty sure that her guests would all come. In about an hour, pants would drop. Then, in about two hours, word would start spreading about the party.

By tomorrow morning, everyone would be coming up to Gin trying to get an invitation to her next party. People she had never even spoken to before would be desperate to talk to her. They'd all be trying so hard not to talk about the party, but wanting more than anything to ask. Maybe she'd even get in with the juniors and seniors. Her life would totally change.

And Sandy would no longer be her only friend.

Sandy looked like she was about to burst with a question, but couldn't bring herself to say it.

"What?" Gin asked as she checked her watch. Her friend was beginning to get annoying . . . well, *more* annoying than usual.

"Why are we doing this?"

"Why not?"

"Well . . . it's just . . . I don't get it."

"What's to get? It's a party."

"But it's not much of a party for us, is it?" Sandy asked. "I mean, the girls are doing all the work. When do we get to have fun?"

"Oh, we'll be having fun," Gin said.

"So they'll . . . you know"—Sandy looked down her body with a nod—"to us in return."

"I highly doubt that."

"Well, if we're not getting anything, why are we doing this?"

"Because it's *fun.*"

"For the boys."

"No. For us, too," Gin said. "Trust me."

"But—"

"You just don't get it," Gin interrupted. "Just wait and see."

She'd never be able to explain the feeling to Sandy. She needed to experience it herself. There was nothing like the feeling of being in total control. Knowing that she was the one determining just how much pleasure the guy was having. Making a guy beg her to let him get off. The moans of pleasure . . . and she was the cause.

"You *really* saw this Rainbow Party thing on Dr. Donovan?"

"Yep," Gin said.

It was the best thing she had ever seen on TV.

Gin wasn't supposed to go out until her parents came home. She wasn't supposed to have boys over, either, but what her parents didn't know wouldn't hurt them. If Gin couldn't find an available guy or convince Sandy to come over, she was usually stuck in the house bored out of her mind. More often than not she wasted time by watching *The Dr. Donovan Show.*

Dr. Donovan was supposedly this expert on everything, even though she was only called a *doctor* because she had a PhD in literature. She would bring on actual experts to talk about anything outside of her area of expertise. As far as Gin could tell, *everything* seemed to be out of the doctor's area of expertise.

"I can't believe Dr. Donovan would tell anyone about these parties," Sandy said. "It doesn't seem like her kind of thing."

Gin laughed. "It wasn't one of her party planning shows. She wasn't doing an episode on 'How to Host a Rainbow Party.'"

"Oh."

"She had some expert on saying how kids were doing it all over the country."

"Really?" Sandy said. "I never heard of it before."

"Me neither. Anyway, the audience was so shocked by it.

They kept cutting to these women covering their mouths in horror. . . . I swear, one woman was even crying."

"The audience does that a lot on her show," Sandy said.

"It was like they didn't know teenagers had sex," Gin said. "They kept going on and on about how *wrong* these parties are and how *evil*."

"Evil?"

"You know how Donovan makes everything *so* dramatic." Gin lifted the back of her hand up to her forehead like she was Scarlett O'Hara from *Gone with the Wind*. "If anyone needs to go to a Rainbow Party, it's Dr. Donovan."

"Well . . . ," Sandy said quietly, "maybe she's right."

"You are so fucking naive," Gin said.

Sandy was really getting sick of GIn talking to her like that. "I'm just saying . . . ," Sandy said. Maybe Gin was used to this, but Sandy certainly wasn't. As far as she was concerned, it was perfectly normal to be freaking out a little. Even Dr. Donovan would agree.

And don't think she wasn't annoyed that Gin didn't answer her question about why they were doing this in the first place. It didn't seem like the girls would be having much fun . . . or any fun at all. In all honesty, it seemed like a lot of work for absolutely no reward. If Sandy didn't know Gin better, she would have figured this was Hunter's idea. But Gin seemed to be all for it.

And Sandy was going right along.

Once again, Sandy wondered what she was doing there. Why did she agree to come?

Rusty.

Oh yeah, that was the reason.

Sandy was worried about Gin finding out she was secretly crushing on Rusty. The last thing Sandy wanted was for Gin to know who she liked. Gin was very dangerous with personal information like that. There's no telling what she would do with it.

Like that time she found out Allison Monroe had a crush on Scott McPherson, the only boy who had the guts to join the Celibacy Club. Once Gin was through with him he had to quit the club. Not that they had actually had sex, but they had gone far enough.

Sandy had her first serious real crush, but she couldn't even tell her best friend. She desperately wanted to talk about it. She was dying to tell someone about how she felt. The way Rusty made her feel just when he walked past her locker. How she couldn't stop thinking about him. That she filled an entire notebook doodling his name. But as much as Sandy wanted to tell Gin about it, she worried far more about what Gin would say . . . and do.

She really needed to look up the word "friend" in the dictionary. Gin couldn't possibly meet the definition.

"I'm sorry I'm so . . ."

"Yeah, whatever," Gin said as they moved into the living room. "I'm not going to say this again. There's nothing to worry about. I do it all the time."

And there it was.

I do it all the time.

It was the first time Sandy actually believed her. Gin *does* do this all the time. Not that Sandy thought all the stories were lies. She just figured that Gin was exaggerating. No one their age could possibly have as much experience as Gin claimed.

Maybe she doesn't.

Maybe she's as nervous as me.

Maybe it's all just an act.

"Help me move the couch," Gin said. "If we're going to do this right we're going to need some space."

And maybe not.

"How much space do we need?" Sandy asked as she grabbed the couch. Gin's living room looked big enough for what they had planned. One row of boys . . . one row of girls . . .

"Just a couple feet. So we're not all on top of each other. Although that could be fun too."

Sandy let the comment slide. She didn't know what Gin was implying, and didn't want to.

They slid the couch back a bit . . . then a bit more once Gin considered the space. It looked fine to Sandy, but what did she know about these things?

What do *I know?*

"That should do," Gin said. "Now help me with the music. We need to set the perfect mood."

"Okay," Sandy said, still wondering why she was going along with Gin's plan. There were much better ways to let Rusty know she liked him.

Gin grabbed her iPod and plopped down on the newly moved couch. Sandy sat close to her friend, leaning over her shoulder to see the small lit screen.

"Are you sure we should play music?" Sandy asked. "We won't be able to hear the garage door."

"We'll keep it low. Quit worrying."

"Sorry," Sandy said as she looked over the scrolling list of songs. "How about something romantic?"

"That's not the mood we're going for."

"Why not?"

"Do you think people are expecting some sentimental crap?"

"Perry probably is," Sandy said. "And Ash. Some of the things he's done for Rose have been way romantic. Like the time he filled her locker with white roses . . . and they sprang out at her like one of those snakes in the cans. Wouldn't you just die if a boy did that for you?"

"Yes. I think I would," Gin said, and not in a nice way. "What do you think is going to happen this afternoon?"

"I don't know," Sandy said defensively. "But wouldn't it be cool if one of the guys came with flowers for all the girls . . . to thank us. Sounds like something that . . . never mind."

She had almost said his name again.

Rusty.

"You need to start thinking about this differently," Gin said, "or you're going to be in for a big surprise."

"But wouldn't it be sweet?" Sandy asked as if she was still playing the idea out in her mind. "You're in a room full of people doing . . . what we're going to be doing . . . your eyes meet his, and you just know you're meant to be together. Forever. Then Jessica Simpson comes on singing 'Take My Breath Away' . . ."

"And he shoots in your mouth."

"Gin!"

"What? That's what's going to happen in an hour."

"Do you have to make it sound so disgusting? Sex should be romantic."

"I think you're confusing sex with making love."

"Aren't they the same thing?" Sandy asked.

"Not at all," Gin replied. "Sex is dirty. It's messy. It's . . . fun. Making love is . . . well, it seems like a lot of work to me."

"Have you ever made love with a boy?"

"God, no. Why would I want to?"

In that moment, Sandy realized that was the main difference between her and Gin. It was sad, really. Sandy wasn't one of those silly girls who expected to fall in love with only one guy and get married to him and live happily ever after. She knew there were a lot of guys out there she could love, and who could love her in return. At least, she hoped there were. But she wasn't like Gin either. She didn't think she could hook up with whatever guy looked her way.

Sandy knew there was a middle ground. Somewhere between slut and virgin-on-her-wedding-night. Somewhere between Gin and Allison Monroe. Even Allison had gone out with boys before. *I'm not even there yet. But to get to that midpoint, I'll have to start somewhere.*

It might as well be in Gin's living room, she thought, still trying to convince herself it was what she wanted.

"I can't wait to make love with a boy. It will be perfect. The music . . . the mood . . ."

"The nausea."

"I think it's sweet."

"Look Sandy," Gin said, pushing aside the iPod. "Save *that* for your wedding night. Guys only want sex. They don't care about that romantic crap . . . the flowers . . . the music. They only do that to get you to bed . . . or the backseat . . . or the locker room . . ."

"Gin!"

"It's true."

"There are guys out there who *do* care," Sandy said. "There have to be. Look at Ash."

"He only does that romantic crap because Rose rewards him for it," Gin explained like she knew everything. "She's probably a bigger slut than me. She's just a one-man slut. At least I haven't let any guys go all the way with me."

Sandy doubted what Gin was saying was true. Rose wasn't the type to use people . . . especially her boyfriend. Maybe Gin didn't really know what she was talking about. That thought gave Sandy at least a little bit of hope that she wasn't the only clueless one in the room.

"How far have you gone?" Sandy asked, honestly curious.

"Far enough," Gin said. "But I'm not a total slut."

No, Sandy agreed mentally. *Not a* total *slut.*

"So you really invited Rose and Ash, hoping to break them up?" Sandy asked. She had realized earlier that that was what Gin had meant when she'd said the thing about adding "spice" to the relationship. Sandy didn't understand why Gin would do that. Rose and Ash made the perfect couple. Sure, they were a bit weird when they were together, but in a cute way. "Do you like him?"

"No," Gin said. "I just wanted to show him that Rose isn't the only girl out there who can give him what he wants."

Sandy couldn't figure out why that was any of Gin's business.

"And you invited Skye so Rod could have some fun too?" Sandy asked.

"The guy's earned it," Gin said. "All that sneaking around he does behind her back just to spare her feelings. Pathetic."

"He cheats on Skye?" Sandy wondered how Gin knew that. Gin had a way of knowing everything that was going on in school.

"That's what I hear," Gin said. "Although I don't really count it as *cheating*. He doesn't go all the way with the girls. He saves that for Skye."

That sounded exactly like *cheating* to Sandy, but she didn't say anything for fear of Gin making fun of her . . . again.

"And Vi?"

"Come on," Gin said. "Isn't it obvious? The girl's got a serious crush on her best friend's boyfriend. I think it's damn nice of me to help her out, don't you?"

And Sandy already knew that Gin had invited Jade in some bizarre popularity power play. That just left one little question:

Why did she invite me?

2:17

Vi glanced at her watch. Only a minute had passed since the last time she checked it, but the constant repetition of checking and rechecking gave her something to do. School had only let out twelve minutes earlier. There was no point going home since she'd only have to turn around and head back in this direction at three.

She couldn't go over to Skye's because Rod was there having some kind of preparty fun. She didn't even want to think about that.

Perry was nowhere to be found, as usual.

Vi considered going over to Gin's early, but she didn't want to have to spend any more time with Gin than she had to. It was still kind of odd that Gin had invited her to the party in the first place. Well, she hadn't really invited Vi directly. Gin had told Skye to tell Vi about it. Vi was used to it though. She usually got invited places through Skye. People often liked to think of them as one unit.

It got really annoying at times.

Vi wondered if she would have even been invited if she wasn't Skye's friend. It wasn't like she really knew Gin all that well. And why would Gin think Vi would be interested in this kind of party in the first place?

The better question is, why am I interested in the party at all?

"Hey Vi!" Rusty shouted as he went for a layup, rolling the basketball off his fingers and into the net.

Vi hadn't even realized her wandering had taken her to the basketball court.

"Hi Vi!" Brick waved as he wiped away some sweat with the sleeve of his T-shirt. "You came by just in time to witness a minor miracle. Rusty scored a whole two points."

"Screw you!" Rusty laughed as he wiped his face with the bottom of his shirt. Vi suspected that he was lifting his shirt to show off his abs.

She didn't mind. It was a nice view.

"Hey are you all right?" Vi asked Brick.

"Yeah. Why?"

"I heard you got hurt in shop," Vi said. Aside from the little Band-Aid on his finger, he looked okay. Maybe she had heard wrong.

Rusty started laughing hysterically, while Brick's face went a little red. "I'm fine. You want to play?" Brick asked, obviously hoping to change the subject. "You and Rusty against me? He could really use the help."

"Once again . . . screw. You."

"That's okay," Vi said. "I'm not in the mood."

Actually, she could use the distraction. She was starting to get nervous about the party, particularly the part about being with Rod. It wasn't her fault that she had feelings for her best friend's boyfriend. It wasn't like she was trying to break them up. She didn't plan the party. What harm would it be to fool around with Rod there? She would even be doing it with Skye's permission.

Then again, if Rod wasn't interested in her, maybe Brick or Rusty would be. She spent so much time hanging with Skye that the only guy she was ever around lately was Rod. Maybe she didn't really like him. Maybe if she spent time with other guys, she'd find something better.

"Come on, we'll play to twenty-two," Brick said. "I'll even spot you twenty points since you're stuck with Rusty."

"Hear this?" Rusty said as he held his middle finger down. "Let me turn it up." He then turned his hand so that his middle finger was raised. It was a lame old joke, but sometimes so was Rusty.

"I'm fine," she said. She didn't want to get all sweaty either. "You guys seen Perry?"

"Not around here," Rusty said. "Ever."

"He's not much into sports," Brick added.

"Well, maybe some sports," Rusty added. "Or sportsmen."

Vi knew what Rusty was trying to imply. She had heard the jokes. They didn't really know Perry. He wasn't that kind of guy at all. Granted, the two of them never really talked about things like that. Sure, she talked to Perry all the time about boys she was interested in. He always listened and told her when she was being neurotic. It was actually nice to get a guy's perspective. Skye usually just agreed with whatever Vi said.

Even though Perry never talked about any girls he liked, Vi knew he wasn't gay. He just couldn't be.

"I haven't seen him all day," Vi said.

"He'll be at the . . . ," Brick started to say.

"At the what?" Vi asked.

"Yeah, Brick. At the what?" Rusty acted like he knew what Brick was going to say. He had this weird smile and a look in his eyes that suggested there was something going on.

That's when it hit Vi . . . like a ton of bricks.

"No," she said.

"No what?" Brick asked.

"He's not going to be at the . . . at the . . ."

"Yeah," Rusty said. "I was shocked too. Looks like ol' Perry's gonna get some for a change. . . . Hey, wait . . . *you're going!* You and Perry!"

"Rusty, knock it off," Brick said. "Look, Vi. I'm sure you don't have to . . . do anything with anyone you don't want to."

"That's not how it works," Rusty said. "The rules—"

"Hey, Rusty, check out the babe in the indigo bikini," Brick interrupted, pointing to the bleachers.

Vi couldn't help but look too. She didn't like what she saw. If there was ever a definition of a perfect body, this was it. Lying out on the bleachers, soaking up the sun, was what could only be described as the hottest girl she had ever seen in her life. Vi didn't recognize her, so she must not have gone to Harding. *Everyone* would know a girl like that.

So, what's she doing lying out on the school bleachers?

Vi wrapped her arms around herself, like she was trying to hide her body. As if anyone was looking at her at the moment.

Brick did glance back at Vi and gave her a nod that she should go. She was relieved that Rusty wasn't going to get the chance to tell her what she was expected to do in an hour. It was one thing to do those things, but it was another thing to have to think about it. She took off quickly, heading back across the fields toward school.

Although she was happy for the distraction, Vi hated the fact that it was so easy for guys to be distracted around her. First Rod, now Rusty. She knew she wasn't gorgeous, but she wasn't so horrible to look at either. The real problem was that Skye was beautiful. Not as beautiful as the mystery girl in the bikini, but pretty hot. Jade was beautiful too. Even Rose was pretty, in an eclectic kind of way.

Vi was just plain. "Average" was the perfect word to

describe her, as far as she was concerned. She wasn't *ugly,* but she was a long way from what she wanted to be.

Vi really should have been best friends with Gin. Sure, Gin could be annoying most of the time, but she was only about a five on the hotness scale. It didn't hurt to surround yourself with people less attractive than you.

She wondered if that's the way Skye looked at her.

Stop it! she warned herself. It was like she had forgotten that Skye was her best friend. Skye never treated Vi like anything other than a friend. And now, Vi was suspicious about everything. And all she could think about was being with Skye's boyfriend.

The party was starting to mess with her head.

It wasn't until she had put the baseball and soccer fields between her and the basketball court that Vi got that nagging feeling that she had forgotten something else. Something that made the party even more of a mistake. One of the guys had said something. . . .

Perry!

Perry was going to be at the party.

Perry—whom she had known since they were in diapers—was going to be there.

Perry—who was the closest thing she had to a brother—was on the guest list.

She had figured that Hunter would go. It was practically guaranteed. This wasn't the kind of thing that Perry would be into, though.

She should have known Hunter would talk him into it. Hunter was always making Perry do things he didn't want to. That's why she hardly hung around Perry at school anymore. But, it would be too weird if he expected her to . . .

It would just be too weird.

"That's it!" she said aloud to no one. "I'm not going! This is crazy. Why would I even consider it?" She realized that she was ranting out loud as she crossed the teachers' parking lot, but she couldn't stop herself. "I mean, what the hell? Really? What. The. Hell?"

Principal Hogan stopped to stare at her as she was getting into her car.

Vi smiled. "Hi, Principal Hogan."

"Is everything all right?" he asked.

"Fine," she said. "Everything's just *fine*."

And for the first time since she got out of bed that morning, everything *was* fine. She wasn't going to the damn party. She wasn't going to let her friends make her do something she didn't want to do.

She was going to go right over to Skye's house and tell her that she wasn't going.

Then, of course, Skye would get mad at her for not going.

Rod would probably be upset too. He did say earlier that he was "looking forward to it."

Gin would probably be angry because it would mean there would be more boys than girls, but Vi didn't care what she thought.

Perry would be relieved. But Hunter would probably use this as another reason to convince Perry that Vi wasn't cool enough to be around. Hunter was always trying to take Perry's friendship away from her like it was some kind of prize. She hardly saw Perry outside of school as it was.

And maybe if she blew off the party she'd also be missing a chance to get with a guy she could fall in love with. Maybe she *would* miss out on her chance with Rod.

Suddenly everything wasn't quite as *fine* anymore.

"Man, I gotta get some of that," Rusty said as he looked over the body of the nearly naked blonde lying out on the bleachers. She looked about their age, but way hotter than most of the girls in their class.

It was his first sunbather of the season. Even across the length of the basketball court, Rusty could tell she was stunning. Her skin already had some color. Her body was slim yet curved in ways to inspire new dreams to pursue at a later, more private, time.

She looks like she's going to need some help putting lotion on her back.

There was a slight stirring in Rusty's crotch that alerted him to the danger of these thoughts. Basketball shorts were not the best choice of clothing to hide certain uncontrollable bodily reactions.

"Dude, what the fuck's *indigo?*" Rusty asked, hoping to take his mind off her body.

"It's like a bluish-purple," Brick replied defensively. "Or a purplish . . . that!" he added, pointing to the girl.

"Don't point," Rusty said, smacking down Brick's hand. "Geez. Grow a brain."

"Sorry."

"Make it look obvious."

"Oh, like your drooling isn't obvious," Brick said.

Like the "Virgin Brick" has the nerve to make fun of me around women.

"She can toss my cookies any day," Brick continued.

See what I mean?

"Toss your *salad,* moron," Rusty corrected. "Toss your *salad.*"

Rusty laughed as Brick went red in the face.

"Let's play," Rusty said, giving a bounce pass to Brick. "Where did Vi go?"

"You just noticed she left?"

"You were the one that pointed out the babe in the *indigo* bikini."

"I thought you'd want to be informed."

"Oh, I did. I did."

"Check this!" Brick said as he made a shot from the three-point line. "Nothing but net!"

Rusty went for the rebound. The ball went up and over the net, hitting the backboard and bouncing right back into his hands.

"Nice one," Brick said.

"I'm saving my scoring for off the court," he said. "Wait

until you get a load of Gin. The girl's a machine," Rusty said, remembering his first time with Gin.

His *only* time with Gin.

He still didn't know why there had never been a repeat performance. Gin never seemed all that selective with her guys. Once she hooked up with a guy, he usually came back for more. Rusty had come back several times and was always turned away. She was always nice about it, but he was still being rejected.

His "reputation" wasn't going to last if he didn't get some more action soon.

Rusty took the ball three feet before Brick stole it from him. He then tried to put himself between Brick and the net. Brick feinted left, then right, then swung past Rusty for the net. Rusty didn't even notice that Brick was behind him.

Rusty's mind wasn't in the game at all.

"Beat that!" Brick said, slamming down the basketball.

"Let's just hope you don't shoot as quickly as you just did," Rusty said.

"Oh, I got much more in me than just one," Brick said.

Rusty took out the ball again.

"Doesn't work that way," Rusty said as he tried to get past Brick. "It's one shot per customer."

"How the hell do you know?" Brick blocked every move Rusty tried to make. "You've never been to one of these things. Hell I never even *heard* of these parties before Gin invited us."

"My cousin told me," Brick said. "He gave me the full details on what to expect."

"This the cousin that played strip poker with the entire girls' swim team? Then did them all . . . one after the other . . . all night long."

"Yep."

"This the cousin that claims he's packing twelve inches that no one has ever seen?"

"Umm . . . yes."

"Somehow I doubt his credibility."

Brick took the ball out again. Rusty let him have it since he had just about given up on the game. Brick's size comment made something click in Rusty's brain. Rusty looked down at his shorts. There really wasn't much of a package down there. Not compared to Brick's, at least. Or the other guys on the basketball team.

Not that he spent a lot of time checking out the guys on the basketball team. But it was pretty obvious the first time they all showered together. Puberty just hadn't caught up with him yet.

He hoped.

Because he didn't want to think about it if he'd done all the growing he was going to do.

Rusty tried to put his little friend out of his mind, but he was busy thinking about something he hadn't realized before. It was one thing for the guys in the locker room to see him. But this afternoon he was going to have to take it out in front of a bunch of girls, too. Knowing his luck, he'd be standing right next to Hunter.

He was legend in the locker room.

Instead of building Rusty's reputation, this party could destroy it.

Brick was about to go up for another one. Without thinking, Rusty bodychecked his friend, sending him to the blacktop. Rusty grabbed the loose basketball and shot.

It bounced off the rim, back over his head, and rolled across the court toward the bleachers.

"What the fuck was that? Tackle basketball?" Brick asked as he picked himself off the ground.

"Sorry."

They both looked over at the basketball. It was resting along the bleachers, right under the girl's body.

"I'll get it," Brick said quickly.

"You know the rule," Rusty said. "The one who lost it chases it."

"Let me know if you need any help."

"I think I can manage," Rusty said with a raised eyebrow.

As Rusty crossed the court he went from cocky jock to quivering mess with each step. All because of the girl in the indigo bikini.

"You look hot," she said as he came up to her.

Rusty wasn't sure if that was a comment on his looks or the fact that he was drenched in sweat.

"Yeah," he said.

Idiot!

"It's warm," he added, stating the obvious.

Fucking idiot.

"I was watching you play."

He was watching her breasts.

"Is your friend teaching you the game?" she asked innocently.

Rusty had been playing basketball for three years. He wasn't about to tell her that. He looked back at Brick, who was shooting layups. At least he didn't have an audience for his idiocy. "We're just messing around," he said.

"Messing around can be fun," the girl said.

Rusty tried to speak, but nothing came out.

"I meant on the basketball court," the girl said with a seductive smile.

"Or in the locker room," Rusty said.

Why did I say that?

But the girl wasn't offended. Actually, she smiled at him again. Then she picked up the basketball and passed it to him. "Have fun."

"Yeah."

Rusty stared a couple seconds longer, then turned and went back to the court. He tried to bring back some of his cocky swagger, but couldn't quite manage it. A girl had never hit on him before. Sure, there was Gin, but she was more direct, less flirtatious. Basically she listed a time and place and told him to be there.

This was something entirely new.

"Nice chat?" Brick asked after another layup.

"Man, she's even more fuckable up close."

"Any chance with her?"

"Yeah, she's into me," Rusty said.

"What's her name?

There was a long, drawn-out silence.

"Loser!" Brick laughed. "You didn't even get her name. Oh yeah, she's into you. I can just hear you now. "'Oh yeah . . . do it . . . Mary . . . I mean Brittany . . . I mean Mildred . . . I mean . . . what's your name again?'"

"Who needs a name?" Rusty asked with a sneer. It was clear to Brick that he was trying to mimic Hunter's patented "sexual innuendo sneer."

He didn't quite get it.

Rusty was almost a joke. The biggest stud on the basketball team, and still a virgin . . . technically. *Rusty* didn't consider himself a virgin. There *was* that time that Gin went down on him . . . that *one* time. Whoever made up that stupid rule that blowjobs weren't sex? As far as Rusty was concerned, any time a guy finishes the job while there's a girl in the room, that should count as sex. She doesn't even have to be touching him at the time.

It *should* count.

So what if he'd let the guys think it happened more than once and gone further than it had. It wasn't like he was totally inexperienced, like Brick. But now he had to live up to that reputation. And it was getting harder and harder to do that every day.

Gin's party would give him a chance to build on his reputation. Afterward, he'd be able to work up the nerve to go for Jade—or maybe that girl on the bleachers.

Maybe they'd hear good things about him from the other girls. Then again, maybe he'd make a complete and total fool out of himself. Once the girls saw him with his pants down, he was afraid they wouldn't have much to talk about.

2:24

Rose checked the clock on the wall for the fourth time in the past two minutes and decided that time was simply moving slower today. Ash had left only fourteen minutes ago and it already seemed like hours. Not that she was in any rush. If Ash had to take forever to do whatever it was he had to do, well . . .

What a shame.

She was having a hard time reading *Le Petit Prince* for French. It wasn't the language that was the problem. It was the picture of *les baobabs.* She never gave a second thought to the drawing of the twisting roots of the trees before. But today all she could see in front of her was something, well, kinda phallic.

Merde.

"Have you heard about this party?" Allison asked as she

burst into the student council office and dropped her book bag on the floor beside Rose.

"Party?" Rose asked, looking up from her copy of *Le Petit Prince.*

"This blowjob party?" Allison said. "Have you heard about it?"

"Blowjob party?" Rose figured if she didn't actually answer, it wasn't like she was lying to her friend.

"Yes," Allison said. "Have you heard about it?"

At this point, Rose was forced to lie. "No?"

"I didn't think so," Allison said. "This is such a Gin Norris kind of thing."

"Gin's throwing a party?"

"Some crazy sex party," Allison said. "Who would go to that kind of thing?"

True, who would?

"How did you hear about it?"

"Steve Jacobs has been going around asking *everyone* about it."

Oh God. Rose was having a hard enough time with the fact that everyone Gin invited was going to know what Rose had done. She wasn't ready for it to spread around the entire school. Then again, she had never let the gossip bother her before. Of course, that gossip had all been false. She wasn't sure if she was ready for true gossip about her.

"Can you imagine?" Allison asked.

Rose had been trying very hard *not* to.

"What kind of idiot girl would go to such a thing?" Allison asked.

"Just because some girls want to fool around, it doesn't make them idiots," Rose said.

"But come on," Allison insisted. "Do you know what happens at this party? The girls all go down on the boys. Then they all leave. That's it. Can you imagine a bunch of boys going down on girls and expecting nothing in return?"

"Maybe the girls *do* get something out of it."

"Such as?"

An appreciative boyfriend? A bit of experience with something they know nothing about? I mean, there is something to be said about having other girls around for support.

Yet Rose said none of those things. Aside from the fact that she didn't want to tip Allison off to the fact that she had been invited, Rose also knew that each of those arguments was incredibly stupid. But when dealing with the topic of sex, Rose had long since learned that logic usually flew right out the window.

Yes. Allison had a really good point. A logical and valid argument. And in Rose's brain, she knew that agreeing to go through with this was a mistake. But there was the tiniest bit of her that was curious . . . even a little excited by the idea. And that tiny part of her was far stronger than every other part of her brain, heart, and body that was screaming at her that it was a stupid thing to do.

Instead of meeting Allison's questions head-on, Rose simply changed the subject.

"You're not going to tell?" Rose asked.

"After last week's health class fiasco?" Allison asked. "I don't need to be the school sex narc. It's bad enough everyone thinks I'm some crazy prude just because I started the Celibacy Club."

"I still don't know why you did that."

"And I still don't know why you won't join," Allison said. "And don't give me that story about keeping pressure off Ash. If he really loved you, he wouldn't care what other people thought."

Rose shot her friend a look.

"Oh my God, I'm so sorry," Allison immediately said. "I'm turning into that crazy prude everyone thinks I am."

"No, you're just . . . motivated by your cause," Rose said.

"Okay, let's try this again," Allison said. "Rose, what's the real reason you don't want to join the club?"

Rose had been dreading this moment. She knew that Allison was going to eventually get around to asking her straight out. But just because it didn't come as a surprise didn't make it any easier.

"Look, it's not that I don't get what you're doing," Rose said. "I just don't think the status of my virginity is anyone else's business."

"But that's not the point," Allison said. "It's kind of like a support group."

"I don't think my virginity needs support either," Rose said. "It's doing fine on its own, thank you."

And yet, here I am planning to go to this "party" because I'm afraid of losing Ash even though he's never given me one reason to worry about it.

Rose pushed that thought out of her mind.

"Well, just—" Allison stopped talking as soon as the door opened and Ms. Barrett, the faculty adviser to the student council, stepped into the office and put her bag down on her desk.

"Hey, Rose. Allison." Ms. Barrett sat at the desk and turned on her computer. "Don't feel like going home yet? Nobody good on TRL today?"

"Yeah," Allison said as she stood up and moved to the door. "Good idea. I should go."

"Allison, wait!" Ms. Barrett tried to stop her, but Allison was already gone.

"I think she had to go somewhere," Rose said, covering. She knew that Allison felt guilty about getting Ms. Barrett in trouble and was too embarrassed to be in the same room with her.

"Rose, can you please tell Allison that it's okay," Ms. Barrett said. "I know she didn't mean for anything to happen."

"No, it's . . ." Rose started to come up with some excuse, but the look on Ms. Barrett's face stopped her. "I'll tell her."

"Thank you."

"So . . . what's up?" Ms. Barrett asked as she logged on to her e-mail.

"Nothing," she replied quickly. "Nothing at all."

Rose didn't like the way Ms. Barrett was looking at her. It was like she *knew.* But that was impossible. How would she know? On second thought, it wouldn't be a huge surprise if she did know. She had this way of finding out things other teachers would never have heard about.

"Speaking of TRL," Ms. Barrett said, "Maroon Five was on the Today show this morning. I taped it, if you want me to bring it in next week."

"What?" Rose wasn't really listening. "Um . . . sure?"

Ms. Barrett glanced at the door. "I'm not expecting anyone, if you want to talk about something."

"I'm fine," Rose lied. She was dying to talk to someone. She knew she could trust Ms. Barrett. She was the one teacher in school that was more of a friend than a teacher. But Gin would kill her if she told about the party.

"You seem a little preoccupied." Ms. Barrett got up and crossed over to join Rose on the couch.

"Do I?"

"This wouldn't have anything to do with a certain party?"

"What?" Rose's back went stiff in shock. "How did *you* hear about it? Does everyone know?"

"How do I hear anything?" Ms. Barrett waved away the question. "I just did."

Rose sat in silence. She hadn't intended to confirm the party. Gin would not like that at all.

"I didn't expect that you were considering going. It doesn't really seem like your kind of scene."

"You're not the first person to say that today," Rose said defensively, thinking back to Jade's earlier comment.

"It's not an insult," Ms. Barrett said. "I just can't imagine why you would do something like this."

Rose chose not to answer. Actually, she didn't really *have* an answer.

"Look," Ms. Barrett finally spoke. "This is none of my business. And I'm not going to give you a lecture on how sex is some evil, horrible thing. It can be fun. And it can be special."

"But we're not talking about sex."

"Oh for crying out loud, when did everyone start redefining sex? When did it become SEX only if and when Tab A inserted into Slot B, but not C?" Ms. Barrett asked.

"Slot C?" Rose said with a giggle. It was also the oddest way she had ever heard anyone talk about sex.

"You know what I mean," Ms. Barrett said. "Who is the genius who came up with these rules? I'm not saying we should go back to a time when boys were too afraid to touch a girl. But how did we fast-forward to it being okay to do 'everything but'? And really, what kind of logic is 'everything but,' anyway? If you can get everything *but* pregnant, then suddenly it's okay?"

Now Rose was getting a little concerned. "Ms. Barrett."

"I'm sorry," she said, catching herself. "Principal Hogan just . . . never mind. You were saying?"

"Um . . . nothing."

"Then I'll shut up."

Unfortunately, Ms. Barrett meant what she said. She stopped talking entirely. She was obviously waiting for Rose to say something.

Rose wanted to change the subject, but considering how emotional Ms. Barrett was about the topic, she was afraid her teacher would think she was an idiot. Rose looked down at her fingernails as she stalled. She forgot that she had painted them in black and white spirals to go with the earrings she wore yesterday.

As long as she got good grades, Rose didn't really care what most teachers—or anyone, really—thought about her. But Ms. Barrett wasn't most teachers. She was more like a big sister. Ms. Barrett was the only adult Rose knew that she had ever run into at a No Doubt concert. Rose *did* care what she thought. She didn't want Ms. Barrett to think Rose didn't know what she was doing.

Even if Rose didn't know what she was doing.

There were certainly reasons why Rose was considering going to the party. Sure, they might not be the most rational reasons in the world, but that was how Rose felt. Should she stop herself from doing something just because other people didn't understand why? Just because *she* didn't entirely understand why?

She finally looked at Ms. Barrett and softly explained her reasoning.

"I'll be making Ash happy."

"For the moment, yes," Ms. Barrett said in a matching soft tone. She had apparently used the silence to calm herself. "But how happy will you be if all you're concerned about is *his* happiness?"

"Ash makes me happy in other ways."

"And I'm sure you make him happy in other ways too."

"Absolutely!" Rose said quickly.

"Then why do either of you need to go to this party?"

Ash started his trek in Aisle 1 of the mall drugstore, dropping a pack of pencils into the red plastic basket he had grabbed on the way in. He was always losing pencils. No matter how many he started the week with, they were all gone by the end. It made no sense at all.

Moving on to Aisle 2, he considered getting a card for Rose. A nice thank-you card for the key chain. But the gift wasn't really thank-you card worthy. And giving Rose a card on this particular afternoon might send the wrong message. She might think he was thanking her for something else entirely. And that wasn't exactly something one would give a thank-you card for.

Was it?

He dropped the card in the basket anyway. It wasn't that expensive. Besides, he needed other stuff to buy. He could always save it for some other time. There would be plenty of opportunities to give Rose a card in the future.

Ash checked his watch. It was almost two thirty. He was going to have to move it if they wanted to get to Gin's on time. Then again, if he got delayed, they wouldn't have to go to the party at all.

Not such a bad thing.

But Rose seemed to want to go for some reason. And he wanted to make her happy.

Leaving Aisle 2, he weaved up and down the store, dropping Tic Tacs, Band-Aids, a toothbrush, condoms, and nail clippers into the basket.

It was a nice little pile of items, but everything was pretty cheap. He needed most of the things anyway. Sure, the Tic Tacs and clippers could wait, but it wasn't like he was wasting money.

Ash hurried up to the front registers. There were two open beside each other with short lines in front of each. One line consisted of several senior citizens with the little bags holding their prescriptions. The other line had more senior citizens as well as a pair of rather hot college girls.

He chose the all-senior-citizens line and checked his watch three times while he waited. Ash and the college girls got to their respective registers at the same time. He dropped his items on the counter and left the basket on the floor.

Don't make a big deal out of the condoms. Don't make a big deal out of the condoms.

The middle-aged woman at the register picked up the

card first and scanned it. Once the register beeped, she put the card to the side so it didn't get wrecked in the bag. Then she scanned the pencils. . . .

Beep

Clippers . . .

Beep . . .

Condoms . . .

No beep.

She scanned the condoms again.

Still no beep.

It figures, Ash thought as his eyes focused down on the edge of the counter. He was already imagining the woman grabbing the P.A.

Can I get a price check on condoms? A pack of condoms for the fifteen-year-old boy at my register?

It happened all the time on TV.

But the announcement never came.

The woman at the register had probably been through this kind of thing before. She discreetly held the box out behind the register and motioned to her check stand partner, a weathered old man who probably had been working at the store since before condoms were even invented. He was just finishing his transaction with the college girls, handing one of them a pen to sign for her credit card purchase.

"Harold, how much are these?" the woman asked.

"Is that the three-pack?" Harold asked.

It was fairly obvious to Ash that he had picked up the three-pack. The six- and twelve-packs of condoms were in boxes over twice the size.

"Three."

"Ribbed, lubricated, or both?" Harold asked.

Ash's face went so red it was almost purple. Thankfully, the college girls didn't giggle. He wasn't sure if they were even paying attention. His eyes were *totally* focused on the edge of the counter.

"Never mind, Harold," the woman said smoothly. "I'll look them up myself."

She bent under the counter and pulled out a binder. Ash could sense the college girls walk behind him and out the store as the woman flipped through the pages. It only took a moment for her to find the price of the condoms.

Ash let out a breath that he wasn't aware he had been holding.

The woman pressed a few keys on the register and dropped the condoms in the bag. She then continued, scanning the Band-Aids. . . .

Beep.

And Tic Tacs.

Beep.

Naturally.

Ash paid for his stuff. He didn't want to wait for the change, but at least the condoms were now hidden in the bag. He almost forgot to pick up the card, which the woman quickly slipped into a small separate bag. Ash stepped out of the store, wiping some sweat off his forehead.

He checked his watch again, but didn't even notice the time. It was more out of habit at this point. Turning right, he headed for the exit.

And ran right into Steve Jacobs.

"Tell me you know about the party," Steve said instead of "hello."

"Party?" Ash asked, trying to come up with some kind of cover story. Without thinking, he held the drugstore bag behind his back. Not that Steve could see what was inside.

"This Rainbow thing," Steve explained. "Just tell me who's throwing it. Come on, man. I know you know."

"What are you talking about?"

"The Rainbow Party," Steve said. "I heard Hunter talking about it earlier. I thought it was dumb that he was excited over some party with a stupid name. But then I looked it up online. It sounds like it's gonna be a blast."

"Sorry, man," Ash said as he pushed past Steve. "Can't help you."

"Some friend you are," Steve said as he took off in the other direction.

We're not even friends, Ash thought.

The last thing Ash needed was for word to spread about this party. It was bad enough that there were going to be other guys there. He didn't need the entire JV football team showing up.

Ash continued for the exit . . . where he saw Hunter and Perry coming in.

This is ridiculous.

Without thinking, Ash ducked into the first store he came to so he didn't have to talk to anyone else about the party. Luckily, it was the bookstore. If he had been ten feet farther, he would have been forced to hide out in the middle of Victoria's Secret.

He entered the store, scanning the aisle for the most logical place to hide.

Children's Books?

No.

Romances?

No.

Gay and Lesbian Studies?

Um . . . really . . . no.

Hunter and Perry were getting closer, so Ash ditched to the side by the magazine rack.

"I told you it was Ass," Hunter said as he and Perry came into the bookstore. "Hey Ass!"

Ash nodded *hello.* He was used to Hunter calling him "Ass." The only thing that bothered him about it was just how unoriginal it was. His "friends" had been calling him "Ass" since the fourth grade.

"Hi Ash," Perry said as they caught up with him.

"Hey."

"Talk about whipped," Hunter said, grabbing a magazine

with a hot celeb in a wedding dress on the cover. "Rose already has you planning the wedding?"

"What?" Ash finally noticed that he was standing in front of all the wedding magazines. "Oh, I was just checking out—"

"Don't have to explain to me," Hunter said. "Nothing hotter than a babe in a tight white dress."

"Who would've thought Hunter Kennedy had a wedding fetish," Perry mumbled just loudly enough for Ash to hear.

Ash laughed at the comment. He figured Hunter missed it because he was so focused on checking out the girls in the magazine. Perry was always coming out with lines like that under his breath.

"Guess Rose won't be wearing white at your wedding, huh?" Hunter said as he dropped the magazine back in the rack.

Ash said what he usually did in these situations.

Nothing.

"Knock it off," Perry said, with very little conviction.

"Looking forward to sampling some variety later, huh?" Hunter said. "Who knows? Maybe you won't want to go back to being a one-woman man."

Ash felt an overwhelming urge to punch Hunter. It actually surprised him. He wasn't prone to violence. He constantly put up with this kind of talk. It had never gotten to him before.

Then it hit him.

Hard.

I love her.

There it was again.

He still didn't know where it came from or why it kept popping up today. With all the thoughts he was having over the party, he had almost forgotten the earth-shattering revelation from an hour ago. *And I wanted to protect her.*

"Hey? You in there?" Hunter asked, snapping Ash back to attention.

"You better watch what you say about the party," Ash warned. "Steve Jacobs is trying to crash."

"Like that loser would even be let in the door," Hunter said. "According to Gin, he's a mess when it comes to sex. Doesn't know what to do with his own equipment, much less a girl's."

"Gin's been with Steve?" Ash asked.

"Man, who *hasn't* she been with?" Hunter asked. "Except for you guys. But that'll change pretty soon."

"You're going, Perry?" Ash asked, trying to deflect attention from himself. It was a given that Hunter would be there, but it wasn't the kind of thing Perry would usually have been into.

"Of course he's going," Hunter said, even though Perry looked a little doubtful. "He'd be an idiot if he didn't."

"Yes, because we all know how the ability to get a blowjob is a sign of intelligence," Perry mumbled. "What with mental agility required for maintaining an erection and all."

"What the fuck are you talking about?" Hunter asked.

Ash was too busy holding back his laughter to hear Perry mumble his apology.

Once he could breathe again, Ash checked his watch. "I have to meet Rose," he said.

"I gotta give you props," Hunter said. "I wouldn't want my girlfriend coming to this thing. Once she gets a load of this"—he grabbed his crotch—"she might not want to go back. Girls have been known to develop an addiction."

Ash wasn't sure what Perry mumbled, but it sounded something like, "Emphasis on the dick."

"I think we'll be fine," Ash said.

"Still . . . never can tell," Hunter said.

"Well, I've got to go," Ash said as he started for the mall exit.

"Tell Rose we said hi," Hunter called after him. "And we're looking forward to seeing her later."

Ash ignored Hunter, but he couldn't ignore what he had said. Maybe that was why Rose wanted to go. It would give her a chance to see what the other guys were like . . . what she was missing.

They had been together since they were thirteen. It was one thing to talk about kids, but what were the odds that they would be together for the rest of their lives? The only people they would ever be with would be each other. Sure, Rose was always talking about how Vi's parents had met in high school and fallen in love, but that was just one example. It certainly didn't prove that he and Rose were meant to be together.

What if she *was* interested in some other guy . . . like Hunter.

Okay, well, she'd never be into a guy like Hunter, but maybe one of the other guys. Was that the reason she wanted to go?

Was she going to dump him on the same day he realized that he was in love with her?

2:33

"I can't wait to get a crack at Rose," Hunter said. He moved down the row to more interesting "reading." The magazines he wanted were on the top shelf in the back of the rack. He had to stretch to get one. Not for long. Hunter's doctor said he hadn't stopped growing yet.

He hoped he was still growing in other areas too. He knew he was already big, but there was nothing wrong with *bigger.*

"You know, sometimes you can be a real jackass," Perry said as he followed. Every now and then Hunter let him get away with saying things like that.

"True," Hunter agreed, picking up a *Penthouse* and flipping through the pages. "Now that's more like it. Check this out." Hunter held out the centerfold for Perry. A smokin' blonde was spread eagle on the page. Perry didn't look all that interested. He was too busy looking around the store. "What would you say? She's a *C*? *D?*"

"Hunter, you're going to get us kicked out of here," Perry said through clenched teeth.

"Chill," he replied. "Like I ever come into the bookstore."

"Well I do," Perry said. "Put that away before the manager sees you."

"Perry, you have got to calm down," Hunter said. Sometimes his friend could be a real buzz kill. "Maybe we can get you to release some of that tension this afternoon."

"Great," he said with very little enthusiasm.

"You're welcome."

"Whatever."

Perry wasn't usually this rude when Hunter did something for him. Hunter thought it was almost like he didn't want to go to the party. Sometimes, Perry confused the hell out of him. There were times Hunter wondered why he even stayed friends with him. But there were other times, many, many other times—forty-seven, if Perry really *was* counting—that it was obvious.

Not that that was the only reason he was friends with Perry. True, it was a great . . . fringe benefit. But Perry was useful in other ways too. He'd never admit this out loud, but Perry helped him out in the girl department . . . not that he needed any.

As weird as Perry could be sometimes, he always had a circle of girls around him wherever he went. It probably had to do with his threat level. It was nonexistent. He was like the safest guy in school. As long as Hunter hung with Perry, he seemed more credible by association. That association had helped him score a surprising number of times.

And he genuinely liked the guy too.

"None of the girls at school look like that," Hunter said as he put back the magazine.

"Airbrushed with implants?" Perry said. "Not exactly how I like them."

"How *do* you like them?" Hunter asked. "We got a wide variety of girls to choose from this afternoon. Maybe you could hook up for once. You know, once the party's over."

"With whom?" Perry asked. "Gin? Jade?"

"They're mine," Hunter replied. "I meant one of the other girls."

"Rose and Skye? Last I checked they were already taken."

"How *taken* do you think they are if their boyfriends let them go to this party?" Hunter asked. "What about Vi?"

"Don't even go there."

"What? You mean you've never—"

"Who else is going to be there?"

"Sandy."

"Not really my type," Perry said. "Who else?"

"Just guys," Hunter said, growing bored. "Come on, let's find Jade."

"Oh, fun," Perry muttered.

Hunter stepped out into the mall. It was a fairly large place. Jade could be anyplace.

"Let's start in Bloomingdale's," he said as he turned to the left. Hunter wasn't a huge fan of shopping, but Jade looked like she only wore the best. Even Hunter knew that Bloomingdale's was one of the most expensive department stores around.

"This is going to take forever," Perry said. "Can't you just wait a half hour for the stupid party?"

"I'm thinking if we run into Jade, I may convince her to have a private party with me."

"And what am I supposed to do while you're having your private party?"

"Maybe I'll let you have her when I'm done."

"Aren't you generous," Perry said.

"I try," Hunter replied. He suspected that Perry was being sarcastic, but that would be just plain rude. Once again he wanted to remind Perry of all that he was doing for him this afternoon.

Damn ungrateful, if you ask me.

"What are the odds we're going to find her?" Perry whined as he followed. "I mean . . . the mall's pretty big. We could walk right by her and never know it. If she's in a dressing room . . . or if she's on a different aisle than us . . . or if she leaves a store right before . . ." Perry trailed off. "Oh look, there she is."

"Where?" Hunter said before he realized how pathetic it was to sound *so* excited.

"There," Perry said, pointing an arm in the direction of the entrance to Bloomingdale's.

Right where they were heading. Boy, Hunter knew his women.

"Don't do that." Hunter smacked down the arm. "Can you be more obvious?"

"Sorry."

Hunter checked her out. Even at a distance she looked *fantastic.*

"God. She's with her mom," Hunter said as he noticed she wasn't alone. "Did she say she was coming here with her mom?"

"I really wasn't paying much attention."

"Then what good are you?"

"I ask myself that all the time," Perry mumbled.

"This could be a problem. I don't really do well around parents," Hunter admitted. "It's like they don't trust me."

"Imagine that."

Hunter moved faster as he tried to keep Jade from getting too much distance. He weaved through shoppers and nearly knocked into a woman who stopped suddenly to look at a pair of shoes in a store window.

Dammit! Signal first, bitch, he thought as he swerved to avoid her.

"Okay, here's the plan," he said.

"Oh goody. We have a plan," Perry said from a few feet behind. He was dragging his feet like he didn't want to help.

"You got a problem?" Hunter asked, stopping by the mall fountain.

"I don't know what you're doing trying to get Jade alone at the mall when you're going to have a shot at her in like a half hour," Perry said.

"Once again, the operative word here is 'alone,'" Hunter said. "Get her in the right mood. Get her alone—"

"In the middle of Bloomingdale's."

"What can go wrong?"

"Gee, I wonder."

"What's your problem?"

"I don't know," Perry said. "Just seems a bit . . . desperate, if you ask me."

"I didn't ask you," Hunter said, getting pissed.

"I'm just saying—"

"Oh, forget it," Hunter spun in his Skechers and went toward the exit. He shot an angry glare at the woman still window shopping for shoes. "Let's just go back to your place and hang until it's time to go to Gin's."

"Fine," Perry said. "But I have to hit the drugstore first."

"Whatever."

Hunter wasn't sure if he was more pissed at Perry for stopping him from hooking up with Jade or the fact that he knew Perry was right. It *was* desperate to make a move on her at the mall while she was with her mom. *Desperate* was for losers like Rod who snuck around with wannabes from other schools so his girlfriend wouldn't find out.

Hunter Kennedy was anything but desperate.

But if he was ever going to be desperate, Jade Lawrence would be the reason. Not many girls told him "no." Not that Jade had ever actually *said* no. She just never played along with his flirtatious games. That in itself was almost unheard of. Girls *loved* to play Hunter's games.

That fact alone made her *far* more interesting.

"Don't take too long," Hunter said as they entered the mall drugstore.

"Wouldn't think of it," Perry said snidely, but hurried off nonetheless.

Hunter worked his way down the fourth aisle, figuring he'd check out what new and exciting products were available. At the end of the aisle was a section of hanging boxes of various sizes and colors. It was amazing the things condom companies were coming up with . . .

Ribbed, lubricated, flavored, colored.

Condoms for *his* pleasure, for *her* pleasure.

Hell, there were even oddly ribbed condoms for *twisted* pleasure.

Whatever the fuck that means.

Hunter felt the women standing nearby before he saw them. He was pretty good at sensing babes in his presence. It was like he had this radar that helped him get laid. He could always tell when a girl was watching him.

This was different. He knew he was being watched, but

he didn't feel that familiar pull that meant he was in for some action.

Hunter looked to his left and shuddered.

Well, that explains that.

Two old broads were standing beside the adult diapers staring at him and whispering. He suspected they weren't talking about how hot he was, though he wouldn't be surprised if they were. Older women usually found him attractive, but this would be disgusting.

No, they were probably scandalized over seeing a boy his age looking at condoms . . . of all things.

And the bitches weren't even trying to hide the fact that they were talking about him.

I think it's time to put on a show, he thought as he bent at the waist to check out the condoms on the bottom row. Typically, he could have knelt, but he knew how good his ass looked when he bent this way. Not to mention the fact that the jeans he was wearing would slide down while his T-shirt rode up, giving the grannies enough of a glimpse of the promised land to set their pacemakers on overload.

"There they are," he said loudly to himself and his audience of two. "Extra large."

Hunter picked up the "magnum"-sized box of condoms as he slowly straightened up. He threw a puzzled look on his face, like he wasn't quite sure if he was up to magnum size. He knew he was above the average of kids his age, but not quite at the magnum yet. But that wasn't the point.

It was all about the show.

Hunter's right hand slid down to his crotch as he considered the large condoms. He peeked to the side and watched the women's jaws literally drop. He stroked himself through his jeans, trying to bring himself to attention.

"I don't know," he said out loud, as if he were struggling to consider the purchase.

He was actually getting turned on by the exhibitionism, and assumed the women were too, no matter how shocked they were acting.

"I wonder," he said as he slowly slid down his zipper and slipped his hand into his pants.

The women audibly gasped as their varicose-vein-covered legs carried them out of the aisle . . . and probably out of the store. Hunter smiled at the thought of giving them a story to tell . . . and a memory to secretly relive.

He still had his hand in his pants and wasn't in a rush to remove it.

Leave it to Hunter to tell me to rush and then disappear, Perry thought as he tromped through the store looking for his friend. He started with the magazines, figuring he'd find Hunter looking at *Maxim* or *Stuff.*

No go.

Then he moved onto the candy aisle because, after sex, Hunter's biggest addiction was chocolate.

Nope.

Perry continued through the store, turning a corner onto Aisle 4. He wasn't surprised to find Hunter staring at a box of condoms. It was a bit weird that he seemed to be fondling himself.

Perry stood at the end of the aisle for a moment, enjoying the show.

Dressed or undressed, Hunter had a body that Perry could only hope to have someday.

Then Perry realized they were in the middle of a store in the middle of the mall and—personal enjoyment aside—this was neither the time nor the place for that kind of thing.

"Having fun?" he asked as he came down the aisle.

"Actually, yeah," Hunter said as he removed his hand from his pants and zipped up.

"I assume there's an explanation."

"Yeah," Hunter said, but didn't provide one. "Did you find what you wanted?"

Perry nodded. He was holding a pack of alcohol swabs and a bag of cough drops.

"An odd combination," Hunter said.

"The swabs are for the nipple ring," Perry said, absent-mindedly rubbing the source of potential infection.

"And the cough drops?" Hunter asked. "You still have that sore throat?"

"Yeah, it won't go away," Perry said. It had been bothering him for over a week.

Hunter put back the pack of condoms he was holding and picked up another. "Here. Get these too."

"When did you start using condoms?" Perry asked.

"Check 'em out," Hunter said as he handed over the box.

"A rainbow of colors," Perry read.

"And flavors," Hunter added.

"Flavors?"

"Strawberry, banana . . . cherry."

"Will lipstick even stick to condoms?"

"Who knows? It's not like we're gonna use them. I just thought we'd get them for Gin."

"A hostess gift?" Perry said, mildly shocked. "Who would have thought you'd be so up on your etiquette."

"My momma raised me to be well-mannered and considerate," Hunter said in a self-mocking tone.

"Lord knows she didn't raise you to be pure and virtuous."

"Thank God."

Perry walked up to the register with the stuff. They had an arrangement that whoever was doing the buying paid for everything. It was one of the few times in their friendship that things were actually equal between the two of them.

Perry stepped in line behind a mother with her half dozen small children. If there was ever a good reason for condoms, it was the crying, fighting, annoying little kids she couldn't even keep track of. One of the smaller girls was pulling at Hunter's shirt.

Even at age four they can't keep their hands off him.

"I'll meet you outside," Hunter said as he pulled the girl's hand off him and made a dash for the exit.

Perry considered jumping in the other line, but it was much longer. He figured most people were avoiding the kids.

It took another minute for the woman to finish the transaction, gather her rugrats, and pull them out of the store, literally kicking and screaming the entire way. Perry stepped up to the counter, where a man who looked old enough to have partied at the end of the Civil War stood waiting. His name tag said HAROLD and his lack of smile said, *I hate kids too.*

Perry put the stuff on the counter. He waited while Harold scanned them and dropped them in the bag.

"What is this?" he asked, looking at the condoms. "We got a run on condoms today? Don't you kids buy comic books anymore?"

The ones that do certainly aren't buying condoms, Perry thought. He didn't bother saying anything.

Perry got his change and his bag and went to meet Hunter out in the mall. He was nowhere to be found. Perry looked down toward Bloomingdale's, but even Hunter wouldn't have abandoned him like that without a word. Since Victoria's Secret was only a couple doors down, Perry figured that's where he was adding fuel for his fantasies.

Perry walked in that direction, but stopped when he saw Hunter coming out of a side hall.

"Where'd you go?" Perry asked.

"Bathroom," Hunter replied as he continued in the direction of the exit.

"Where to now?" Perry asked as he fell in step with Hunter.

Hunter's eyes were drawn to the Victoria's Secret window. Then he made a quick glance back toward Bloomingdale's.

"Not again," Perry said.

"Let's go back to your place," Hunter replied, finally looking at Perry. "Get ourselves ready."

Perry wondered what Hunter meant by that. He certainly couldn't have been up for a repeat performance of their hookup in the men's room. Not right before the party. Hunter could go several times in a day, but it seemed to be pushing it with back-to-back action like that.

Not that Perry would have minded in the least.

"Man you are going to have a blast," Hunter said, obviously thinking ahead. "That Gin has got a mouth on her."

"Really," Perry said with both a lack of interest and a slight feeling of jealousy.

"Well, not compared to some," Hunter added. "But she'll do for a girl. It's not like she has the same equipment and knows how to treat it. Girls are different."

"So I've heard," Perry said noncommittally. "Not that I've seen any live examples up close and personal."

The closest he had come to being naked with a girl was back when his mom used to bathe him with their family friend, Vi, when they were four. Otherwise, he had certainly seen enough pictures in the *Playboys, Penthouses,* and *Hustlers* that Hunter snuck out of his dad's sock drawer.

Perry wasn't a fan of the female anatomy. Breasts were one thing. They actually looked nice in a soft and cushiony sort of way. But the stuff going on . . . down there . . . was not all that pleasant to him.

"Well I've seen it," Hunter said. "Closer than I wanted to, but Gin was bitching about not getting anything in return. . . ."

Perry stopped, frozen in front of the Dots ice-cream stand.

"Excuse me?"

"Well, come on. I mean . . . I kind of owed her."

"You went down on Gin!" Perry said *way* more loudly than he had intended.

A pair of soccer moms nearby turned in their direction. Their eyes bugged out, and one of them actually covered her mouth in shock. The women immediately started whispering to each other and pointing at Hunter, even though Perry was the one who had made the outburst.

"Would you like to broadcast it on the P.A.?" Hunter asked. "What did you expect? You knew I hooked up with her a lot. I only did her the one time. I didn't even like it. What's the big deal?"

"Nothing," Perry said, thinking back to Hunter's forty-seven promises of owing Perry *one.* He kind of always knew that Hunter was just stringing him along. Hunter had made it clear that he didn't feel the same way, but there was always the glimmer of hope.

Finding out that Hunter went down on Gin pretty much blew that hope out of the water. Sure, Hunter was talking her up today because of the party, but he was usually bitching about how he didn't really like her all that much. How she would never shut up. How she kept acting like they should start dating.

Was it all just an act?

Did Hunter really like Gin? Perry always assumed that Hunter had been using her to get what he wanted. It wasn't like Perry wasn't aware that Hunter was doing the same thing to him. But the difference was that he and Hunter were friends. Best friends. Hunter *had* to care more about him than he did a slut like Gin.

Didn't he?

2:36

Rod wasn't sure how he had gotten himself into this position.

It had started out innocently enough. They had just gotten to Skye's house after school. There was over a half hour until Gin's party and he still wasn't sure if they were going.

Skye had told Vi to come over at three, so things were looking good. But she simply refused to tell Rod what was up. He had even started to consider just going on his own and not give a damn what she said. But before he just blew her off, Rod had given it one more try. He started things off by making out with her on the living room couch.

If only he had known at the time where he would ultimately end up.

"I didn't even know you and Gin were friends," he had said as he broke their kiss.

"We're not," Skye replied. "Not really. As far as I know,

Sandy's her only real friend. Gin probably thinks this is some kind of way for her to make friends."

"Well, then, it was very nice of her to ask us," Rod said. "Don't you think?"

"She's a real sweetheart," Skye said.

Rod laughed and was happy to see that it made Skye smile. He went in for some more kisses, pressing his body up against her to let her know how excited she made him.

After another minute, he broke apart again. "Why do you think she picked us?"

"I think she wants to get her hands on you," Skye said, with a playful kiss. "It's like she's working her way through all the boys in the class."

"Well, this will be the only way she'd get me," he said. "I would never go for Gin Norris on my own."

"Damn right, you won't."

Another kiss.

"But . . . ," he said, pulling away again.

"But what?"

I was just thinking . . . it might be kind of fun for us."

"You've already made that abundantly clear," she said, separating from him. "Between the notes, the e-mails, the text messages. I got the point."

"No," he said, leaning in. "I mean, for us together. Don't you think it's kind of kinky? Like that night we did it in the bleachers. Anyone could have seen us."

Rod was taking a risk on this one. He wasn't really sure

how wild Skye liked it. She seemed to enjoy herself that night on the bleachers. He knew *he* did.

"It might be fun," she said.

"It might even bring us closer," Rod said. "Be good for our relationship." He knew that girls always liked it when guys talked about their "relationship."

"Maybe."

"I'm not just thinking about me," he said. That was true. He was thinking about Gin and Rose and Sandy, and especially Vi. "I'm thinking about us. I want to do this for you, too."

Well, if you really want to do this for me," she said.

"Of course I do," he replied.

"Then there's something else you could do for me too."

"Anything."

Anything.

It was such a simple little word. If only he'd known what it had meant at the time. But he really was willing to do anything for her . . . anything that would get him to the party.

And that's how he found himself in this incredibly awkward position.

"Lower," Skye whispered breathlessly. "Lower."

The *breathlessly* part was just for effect. She wasn't really feeling all that breathless, but she was trying. If only to encourage Rod.

"Lower!" she insisted.

"Sorry," Rod mumbled, sounding more annoyed than apologetic.

She certainly hadn't expected things to progress this way when she suggested it. She hadn't even planned to ask. The words sort of came out of her mouth. It was just another way for Skye to stall on making the decision about the thing at Gin's. But this way she could let Rod ultimately make the decision. If he went along with what she suggested, then they'd go. If not, he'd go home.

She never actually imagined he'd go for it. He certainly never took it upon himself to do it before.

"OH! There!" she said quite loudly and nowhere approaching *breathlessly.*

Although he hadn't reached the target, she'd be happy to wait while he figured out what to do now that he was in the vicinity.

The clock radio on her mom's nightstand indicated they had plenty of time to explore. Gin's house was only a couple blocks away. Besides, maybe she'd make him forget about the party altogether.

Right. Like that would happen.

Skye closed her eyes and let her other senses take over.

The feel of Rod's body as she experienced new sensations. The sounds of her simulated moaning. The taste of Rod's kisses still lingering on her tongue.

The scent of sex.

Well, not actually sex, but a reasonable facsimile.

"That's it," she said encouragingly, even though it wasn't quite . . . it.

She had to give him kudos for trying. He was the persistent little trooper. Considering he'd never offered to do this before.

Rod must really want to go to the party. Skye worried that maybe she was about to make a mistake.

She ran her hands through his golden blond hair, gently guiding him to the exact spot.

That's better.

"I think somebody's going to get to go to a party," Skye said. Mistake or not, Rod had gone along with the plan. It was the only right thing to do. At least, that's what she tried to convince herself. Once again, she wasn't thinking with her brain.

He popped his head up. "Really?" Rod asked with a level of excitement bordering on a child at Christmas. But Skye was the one getting the present. "I love you," he said.

"Don't stop," she instructed.

Leave it to Rod to totally ruin the mood. Saying *I love you* when *thanks* would have done fine. She almost considered telling him to stop because she had changed her mind, but why would she punish herself?

Instead, Skye allowed herself to believe that Rod *did* love her. He was certainly trying to make her happy. Wasn't that more important than any empty promises of love? She almost let herself believe it. He *was* making her feel really good at the moment.

And while she let herself believe that, she also wondered about the guys *she* would be making feel good in a short time. It was possible that one of them could make up for the things she was missing in her relationship with Rod.

If she only knew what it was that she was missing.

A car pulled up in front of the house, taking Skye out of the moment. She checked the clock again. It was way too early for her mom or stepdad to be home. Her brother, Mark, had classes until late in the afternoon. Considering that her stepsister, Vicki, was only five, and didn't know how to drive, the odds were pretty good that it wasn't her either.

She almost said something to Rod about it, but there was no way she was stopping him. He was really getting into it. Besides, there were cars going up and down the street all day. The driver could very well be stopping by to visit a neighbor.

Even so, she slid her hand down the length of her body to help hurry things along.

"Oh yes," she said more to spur Rod along than for any genuine need to express herself.

She thought she heard the front door open.

"Did you . . . WHOA!"

That moan had been genuine . . . and totally distracting. The sudden rush stimulated all the nerves in her body. She was getting close. So close to having her first, very own, non-self-stimulated orgasm.

The feeling was very different than the times she had

been alone in the tub. All her nerves were tingling. The few times she and Rod had had actual full-on sex she had never gotten this close. This was the first time they were focusing entirely on *her* needs. And her needs were about to be met. "Faster," she instructed.

Her breathing intensified. She grabbed a clump of the comforter in her hand, squeezing tightly. She was feeling all those things she had read about in the trashy romance novels her mom kept hidden under the bed they were on. Skye's bosom heaved. Her loins burned with desire. Waves of pleasure washed over her body ready to crash on the shore.

She was ready to explode.

She was . . .

"Skye!" a small voice yelled from the other side of the door. "What are you doing in Mom's room?"

Coitus interruptus in the form of a five-year-old.

But she wasn't alone.

"Skye?" Mark banged on the door. "Why's the door locked?"

"Shit," Skye whispered.

Rod was frozen between her legs. So close, and yet . . .

Skye was amazed as she watched Rod fly off the bed and grab his pants. She knew he could move on the football field, but she had never seen this before. Then again, he didn't have the same motivation on the football field.

"What do we do?" Rod asked, softly but urgently.

"I don't know," Skye replied as she got up and quickly threw on her clothes too.

This was so not good. Being caught by Mark was only a step down from being caught by her mom. He probably wouldn't say anything, but he would definitely find a way to make sure Rod never came into the house again.

Still shirtless, Rod went to the window, slid it open, and stuck his head outside.

"What are you doing?" Skye whispered.

"Looking for an escape route."

"There's nothing there," she said. "You'd kill yourself before you could make it to the tree."

"Better I die on my own than have Mark do it," Rod replied.

"Skye, open the door!" Mark yelled again.

"Skye, don't open the door," Rod insisted.

Like she was about to open the door.

Skye searched the room for a place to hide Rod. In the closet and under the bed just seemed so obvious. The room was so clean that there wasn't anything he could hide behind, under, or in. She didn't know what to do. It wasn't like they could stay locked in the bedroom all afternoon. Mark wasn't going to go away. And they couldn't stay in there until her mom got home.

"Sit down," Skye said, pointing to the chair in the corner. "And act natural."

Skye walked over to the door and took a deep breath as she opened it.

Mark stood in the doorway looking pissed at his sister. He

looked even more pissed once he checked out the room and his suspicions were confirmed.

Vicki was standing beside him. She just looked confused by all the yelling.

"Hey, Skye," Vicki said as she dashed into the room and hopped on the bed. "Hi, Rod!" Her eyes lit up. She had a little crush on him. "What are you doing in Mom's room?"

"Playing house," Skye said quickly. It was a stupid thing to say, and she regretted it the moment it came out of her mouth. Mark looked even angrier. If that was possible.

"Can I play?" Vicki asked as she stood up and bounced on the bed. Where they had just hooked up.

"Some other time," Skye said.

"Skye. We need to talk," Mark said, glaring at Rod.

"What are you doing home so early?" Skye asked, attempting to stall. She walked over to her sister. It never hurt to hide behind an innocent child. "Is Vicki okay? She should be in playgroup."

"My afternoon classes were cancelled," Mark explained. "So I picked her up early. But enough about me. What was going on in here?"

Rod got up and took Vicki by the arm as she bounced up and down. The bedsprings were squeaking wildly. "Let's go play downstairs."

"Okay," Vicki said. Her whole face lit up as she grabbed hold of Rod's hand and bounced onto the floor with a thud.

"You're not going anywhere," Mark said as he put a hand on Rod to stop him.

"Mark!" Skye and Vicki yelled in unison.

Mark removed his hand from Rod's chest and softened his tone. "Vicki, why don't you go downstairs and eat your Chicken McNuggets before they get cold."

"Nuggets!" Vicki cheered, and dashed from the room.

Obviously her love for McNuggets outweighed her feelings for Rod.

"Mom's not going to like her having a snack before dinner," Skye said. She was going for calm, but her trembling voice probably gave that away.

"I think Mom's going to have other things to worry about."

Rod decided to chime in. "Mark, look—"

"I think it'd be best if you shut the fuck up," Mark said.

"Don't talk to my boyfriend like that," Skye said.

"Don't sneak him into Mom's room," Mark said. "What's with that, anyway?"

"What's with what?"

"Mom's room," Mark said. "Why did you bring him in here?"

"Vicki and I share a room," Skye explained. "*And* the door doesn't have a lock."

"Ever think there might be a reason for that?"

Skye tried to come up with an innocent explanation for why they were in her mom's room with the door locked, but none came to mind. Skye knew she'd been caught. Mark wasn't dumb enough to believe any lies she could come up with.

The phone rang.

Saved by the bell, Skye thought as she went to answer it.

"Let the machine get it," Mark said. "We're not done."

Skye knew she'd better do what he said. Unlike her, Mark wasn't the type to deal with things later. He'd want answers now. She was entirely out of options. The only thing she could do was throw herself on his mercy. "Don't tell Mom," Skye said. "Please."

"That you were having sex in her bed?"

"We weren't having sex," she said quickly. "Not exactly."

"Not exactly?" Mark said. "What does that mean? Never mind. I don't want to know."

"It's just like when you and Stacy would be up in your room," Skye said, using what little bargaining power she had. It didn't help that the only thing she could use was from two years ago. "Like I didn't know what you two were doing when Mom was at work."

"That was different," Mark said. "We were sixteen."

"Haven't you heard?" Skye asked. "Fifteen is the new sixteen."

"Very funny," Mark said. "Besides, I'm a guy."

"And Stacy is a girl," Skye reminded him. Thankfully, he gave her something to work with. "So, what you're saying is that it's okay if your girlfriends fool around, but not your sister?"

"That's *exactly* what I'm saying," Mark said.

"You hypocrite!"

"Call me whatever the hell you want," Mark said. "I'm still responsible for you."

"Like hell you are," Skye said. "I can take care of myself."

There was a momentary standoff, and they stared each other down.

While they were both trying to calm themselves, Vicki came into the room with barbecue sauce dripping off her chin.

Mark took one look at her and grabbed a tissue off the nightstand to wipe her face. "I thought I told you to go downstairs and eat."

"Mom's coming home," Vicki said.

Skye's heart dropped. Her mom rarely came home from work early on the spur of the moment.

"You answered the phone?" Skye asked as she knelt beside her sister.

Vicki nodded proudly. Answering the phone was a new thing for Vicki. Skye had forgotten all about it.

"Why is Mom coming home early?" Mark asked, looking up at Skye. It was suddenly clear that he wanted to avoid this almost as much as she did. "Did she say?"

"Nope."

"What did you tell her?" Skye asked.

"Nothing," Vicki said innocently. "Just that you wouldn't let me play house with you and Rod."

"You told Mom we were playing house?"

"Yep," Vicki said as she took a bite of the McNugget that was still in her hand. "Locked in Mommy's room."

Skye looked at Mark. The fight was over. They both understood the situation perfectly. Skye was screwed.

2:48

"How about . . . this?" Jackie Lawrence said, pointing at a bright, shiny, chrome cappuccino maker.

"Once again, *Mom,* we're going for functional, not frivolous," Jade said innocently. Jackie really did not like to be called *Mom.* But Jade enjoyed watching her mother cringe.

Jade knew she was being passive-aggressive by pulling the Mom card, but she couldn't help it. She was getting tired. And they hadn't even been at it for fifteen minutes.

This shopping trip was at the bottom of the list of things to do on Jade's Palm Pilot that afternoon. She usually loved to shop, although she preferred Macy's to overpriced Bloomies. But this wasn't so much a shopping trip as an intervention. And she wasn't even doing it for herself. She was only there for her sister.

Who wasn't even there.

"Not everything has to be practical," Jackie said as she hit the bar code with the scanning gun. "Jenny deserves some fun."

If she had had a little less fun, we might not be here in the first place, Jade thought.

"We need a few fun things," Jackie continued. "Gifts that make this wedding a joyous occasion. Our way of welcoming Toby into the family."

"I think that happened when he knocked Jenny up," Jade said under her breath.

"What was that, dear?" Jackie asked as if she hadn't heard, because she was distracted by Fiesta Ware dishes. "Oh, that is so tacky."

"I don't know, *Mom,*" Jade said, considering the display.

"Please stop doing that."

"Sorry."

"Come along," Jackie said as she moved past the plates. "To China and Crystal."

"Actually, I think Jenny likes Fiesta Ware," Jade said, trying to hang back at the display for a moment. The earthenware tones weren't exactly Jade's thing, but they weren't there for her at the moment. "Haven't you ever seen the crazy colors she decorated her dorm in? This would be perfect."

Jackie looked horrified . . . both at her daughter and at the colorful plates, bowls, and assorted extras. "Why don't we focus on a nice china pattern?"

"But Jenny doesn't need china," Jade insisted. "She *needs* to set up an apartment with her new husband and new baby."

"Why are you set on embarrassing me in front of the salesgirl?" Jackie asked in a tense whisper. Jade looked back over at the woman who had helped set up the scanning gun for them to use for registering gifts. The woman was way out of earshot, as far as Jade could tell.

"Why are *you* set on getting Jenny stuff she doesn't need?" Jade asked, though she already knew the answer to the question. It was the same reason Jenny didn't bother to come along on the trip to fill out her own bridal registry. Whatever Jackie wanted, Jackie got. And what Jackie wanted more than anything was to throw a wedding with all of the appearances of making the marriage look sacred, not shotgun.

"Jenny doesn't know what she needs," Jackie said. "I thought that's why you came along with me."

Well, that was partially right. When Jenny said that she was going to spend the afternoon looking for a part-time job instead of helping Jackie put together the bridal registry, Jade had figured she'd better go along to make sure her sister got at least a few things that she would need. Now, Jade realized that was never going to happen, which is probably why Jenny had found a more productive way to spend the afternoon.

What a good idea.

"You know what," Jade said. "You're right. A wedding should be a special event, and the gifts should reflect that. I don't know what I was thinking."

"I'm glad you understand," Jackie said as she moved away from the Fiesta Ware.

"And it looks like you know what you're doing," Jade said. "I'm just getting in the way. Why don't I meet you back at home?" She started moving off.

"Jade?" her mom stopped, confused.

"I can walk," Jade replied as she continued out of the department without looking back.

Jade didn't know why she even bothered. It was just that she wanted everything to be perfect for her sister. She knew Jenny was stuck in a bad situation. Even though Jenny was her big sister, Jade still liked to look after her.

Jade liked to look after everyone. And she hated it when things didn't work out the way she wanted.

She tried to put the problem out of her mind. Shopping was usually a more soothing activity. That's why she was heading for the Young Miss department two floors down. She knew the perfect way to calm her nerves.

"Umm . . . Jade?" a voice to her right said as she stepped off the escalator.

Jade turned to see a boy from school beside her. It was Steve . . . something. "Hi!" she said.

"Hi, Jade," he said. "How are you?"

"Fine," she said. "You?"

"Good."

Awkward pause.

Jade was trying to remember what classes she had with Steve what's-his-name, so that she could come up with something to talk about, but she wasn't sure they actually had any classes together. He was one of those people she just tended to see in the halls. They'd probably never even said "hi" to each other before.

"I was wondering . . . ," he finally said.

Then another awkward pause.

Jade feared the worst. "Yes?"

"I was wondering," he continued. "Did you hear about . . . are you going to . . ."

Here it comes.

Jade figured he was about to ask her to the Spring Fling.

"I was just . . ." He looked a little sick, as far as Jade could tell. "It's nothing. You're probably not going. I'll see you later."

All Jade could do was stare as he hurried off.

That was weird.

Jade was glad that he hadn't asked her out. She wasn't in the market for a guy right now. Besides, she couldn't even go to the Spring Fling because it was the night before her sister's wedding.

At the same time, she was a bit disappointed. No guy from Harding had ever asked her out before. Oh sure, there was Hunter, but he wasn't really interested in dating her, just nailing her.

Jackie said it was because boys didn't like strong girls like Jade. That was crap, as far as Jade was concerned.

Jade moved on to Juniors. She still wasn't sure what she was wearing to the wedding. Since there were no bridesmaids, Jenny said that Jade could pick out whatever she wanted to wear as the maid of honor. Jade hadn't intended to go dress shopping at Bloomingdale's, but she wasn't exactly shopping for a dress there either.

Her favorite salesguy would be on soon.

Jade figured they had hired him to bring in the customers. He was certainly the main reason she kept coming back to the store.

Considering it was prom season, the dresses overwhelmed the floor. She easily found the dress section before she found the guy, but she kept an eye out for him while she shopped. With her attention split, she had a hard time finding a good dress. It didn't help that their selection was pretty lousy.

Everything was so skimpy; strapless, with slits all the way up the leg or deep down the back. Not to mention how expensive it was for such little material. Current outfit aside, Jade didn't traditionally like to wear such revealing clothes. She just didn't like to be told that she couldn't wear what she wanted. The perfect dress for her was sexy, revealing, but kept some things to the imagination.

A shiny coral number fell into her hands. She wasn't much for coral, usually, but it was her sister's favorite color.

She found the dress the same time she found her salesguy.

Jade caught him out of the corner of her eye as she held the dress to her body in front of a mirror. It didn't take much of an imagination to put her in the outfit, since she almost had enough exposed flesh to make it look like she was wearing it. She tugged on her skirt a little so it wasn't so hiked up. This was the most uncomfortable she had felt all day.

The expression on the saleguy's face implied that he didn't mind. It was so cute how he was trying not to stare while he helped a woman and her ten-year-old daughter. Jade couldn't see his nametag from across the floor, but she knew it said MICHAEL.

He looked more like a Mike, to her.

Once Mike finished with the woman, he came over to Jade. "May I help you, ma'am?"

"Why yes," she said, loving the *ma'am* part. "What do you think of this dress?"

"Personally, I'm not crazy about the color," he said. "But I'm imagining you wearing it . . . and I have to say that it works for me."

"Maybe I should try it on," she said. "Then you wouldn't have to use your imagination."

"Or maybe it would give me something else to imagine," he said with the kind of smile that made the line sexy instead of repulsive. Hunter Kennedy would never be able to pull off a smile like that.

"Which way is the dressing room?" she asked as if she hadn't been shopping at Bloomies for years.

"Follow me," Mike said, leading her around the racks. "Please let me know if you need any help."

Jade leaned in to read his tag as if she didn't know his name. Her face came up within inches of his. "Michael?"

"Yes."

"I think I need some help."

She held the hanger in front of her and used it to lead him into the dressing area with her.

3:00

3:00

"Right this way, ma'am," Mike continued as he took the lead, walking past several open dressing rooms to the very last one. He politely held the door for her as she stepped inside. "Will that be all?" he asked.

In response, she grabbed him by his tie and pulled him into the dressing room with her, locking the door behind them.

"Oh, I'm sorry," she whispered so no one in the other dressing rooms could hear them. "I think I wrinkled your tie."

"That's okay," he whispered back. "It's been through worse."

"It's such a nice tie. Did your girlfriend get it for you?" Her hand was sliding up and down the length of silk.

Mike didn't answer the question, but he quickly looked away from her, which told Jade what she already knew.

"That's okay," Jade said as her hand went up to his chest. "What she doesn't know won't hurt her."

She moved her hand behind his head and pulled him toward her.

The kiss was intense. Lust combined with the possibility of being caught was more than just erotic. Her own adrenaline was an aphrodisiac.

Mike finally ended the kiss. "Ma'am," he said, trying to catch his breath. "We should stop. I could get in trouble."

"Something tells me you like trouble." Jade pulled him into another kiss, prying open his lips with her tongue.

They stayed locked like this for another minute while tongues danced together. It felt good after the grief of dealing with her mom. All that mattered to Jade was what was happening in the moment. There was nothing outside the dressing room.

Unfortunately, Mike had to end the moment too soon.

"No, seriously, Jade," he said. "I could get fired."

Jade pulled back and straightened what there was of a skirt. "I'm sorry."

"You are not." Mike smiled, giving her a quick kiss.

"True," she admitted. "But can you blame me? I haven't seen you all week."

"I know. But I need the extra hours at work right now. Prom can get expensive, even when it's just the junior prom."

"You guys should have it in the gym like we do with the Spring Fling."

"The Cromwell Prep Junior Prom held in a school gymnasium?" Mike acted as if it was a scandalous suggestion. "What would the Alumni Board think?"

"That their kids already go to a school that costs more money than most colleges."

"Daddy's quarterly bonus has to be put to good use," he said. "Well . . . *other* daddies' bonuses have to be put to good use. My daddy appreciates the value of 'a good day's work.'"

"Which is why I don't go out with other daddies' boys," she said. It was true. Jade's dad started working when he was twelve. Of course, Jackie wouldn't let *her* daughter get a "real" job, but Jade filled her time working at the animal shelter and finding other things to keep her busy. "But I *do* miss you," she continued.

Mike looked at her with concern. She knew that she had put a little too much emotion into how much she missed him.

"You're here with your mom, aren't you?" he asked, correctly summing up the situation in a mere moment.

"We're doing Jenny's registry," Jade said, getting upset again. "Jackie's driving me insane. There's nothing on it that Jenny needs. She and Toby are going to be out on their own with nothing but a cappuccino maker and an über-expensive set of china."

Mike put an arm around her. "It's great that you care so much, but don't let Jenny's problem overwhelm you. She's smart. She'll figure it out."

"I know," Jade said. "But she's got so much going on right now. This is just one more thing."

"We've got a pretty good return policy," Mike said. "She can take everything back and get what she needs."

"I guess," Jade said, sighing deeply. She was already starting to feel better in Mike's arms. It was nice to have someone take care of her for a change . . . and she didn't need to be a damsel-in-distress for it to happen.

"Can you go out tonight?" he asked. "Maybe get a bite to eat? You *are* unnaturally thin."

"Can I help it that I have a fast metabolism?" Jade asked. She knew most girls hated her for it, but Jade really did have a problem gaining weight. Not that she considered it a huge problem.

"I'm here until ten o'clock," he said. "Sorry it's so late."

"A late date is better than no date at all," she said.

"Then we're on." Mike started for the dressing room door, but didn't open it. He paused for a moment, like there was something on his mind.

"What?" Jade asked.

"Nothing."

She leaned into him. "Don't play games. What is it?"

"Well," he reluctantly said, "you didn't wear that to school today, did you?"

"What? You don't like it?" She opened her jacket and spun quickly, giving him a flash of underwear.

"No! That's not it," Mike said. "*I* like it. I don't know how

I feel about you wearing it in front of anyone else. It's kind of . . . you look kind of . . . well . . . like a . . ."

"Slut? Tramp? Ho?"

"Three very good word choices."

"Remember my new mission?"

"The dress code!" he said, finally getting it. "That's right. I forgot. How'd it go?"

"It took almost the entire day to get sent to the office! This is going to be easier than I thought. Unfortunately, I didn't have time to change after school."

"You are so . . . unique."

"Yet another reason why you love me."

"Absolutely," he said with a kiss. "So what's the plan for the afternoon?"

"Nothing special," she said.

"Wasn't there some kind of party?"

Oh, that's *what Hunter meant!* She was surprised that Gin's whatever, "Rainbow Party," had gone out of her mind so quickly. She was even more surprised that Rose had said she was going.

Jade stared at Mike, waiting for him to remember the full story.

"What's with the face?" It took a moment, but Mike answered his own question. "Oh, that's right. It's that freak Rainbow thing. You're not allowed to go, by the way."

"Like I would even consider it," she said. Normally she would *never* let anyone tell her what she could or could not do, but Mike was different. She also knew he was just playing with her. He was fully aware that she never had any intention of going.

"You should get back to work," she said.

"Yes, I should," he said, and gave her a quick kiss before leaving the dressing room.

Jade stayed behind to try on the dress. Not only did she want to see what it looked like, she also wanted to give him some time to get back on the floor. It wouldn't look too good to his manager if he and Jade came out of the dressing room together.

Jade checked herself out in the mirror and liked what she saw.

Maybe coral is my color.

The dress looked great on her body. It draped where it was supposed to drape and clung where it was supposed to cling. She would look great at the wedding . . . and at Mike's Prom. Since she looked so good in the dress, she might as well wear it to both events.

Jade imagined wearing the dress on the night she and Mike finally made love. She pictured herself slipping out of it in front of him . . . and standing before him totally exposed. The smile on her face made the dress look even better on her.

Not that they hadn't seen each other without clothes before. They had certainly fooled around, but they had never actually done it. She just wanted to make sure she was ready first . . . contrary to popular belief.

Jade was always amazed at how gossip spread around Harding High. The scary part was most of the things she heard were usually true . . . except when they were about her. Just because Jade didn't buy into all the stupid politics, people started making up crazy stuff about her. Like the fact that she slept with a ton of college guys. Mike was the oldest guy she had ever been with, and he was just a year older than her.

That's why she never bothered to tell anyone at Harding about him. Not even Rose. She liked what they had and didn't want anyone to ruin it for her.

As Jade smoothed out the dress, she took a good look at herself in the mirror.

Jade decided a few weeks ago that she was ready to have sex on his Prom night. She knew she loved him, but wasn't sure she was "in love" with him. They probably weren't going to be together through college, but they were together now and he made her happy.

Not only was she emotionally prepared, but she was physically prepared too. The benefit of having a sister with an unexpected pregnancy meant that she got to go on the pill way before she normally would have.

And she knew Mike was so excited about it that he had already bought the condoms. It wasn't his first time, but that didn't make it any less special.

She wasn't ready to be an aunt . . . there was no way in hell she was prepared to become a mom.

3:01

The first floor hallway was empty. Not even the NTAs were still around. School had been out for an hour. With the exception of extracurricular activities, everyone had gone home.

It had taken Ash much longer to get back from the mall than he had anticipated. It didn't make much sense since the mall wasn't that far away. He had just been walking slowly, as if his feet knew something his mind wouldn't accept.

Ash pulled the pack of condoms out of the drugstore bag. He quickly slipped them into his front pocket with his house keys that were already on the key chain Rose gave him earlier. Then he threw the bag in his locker and shut it. The slamming door echoed through the hall.

He thought back to when he had slammed himself into a

locker earlier. His life had been much easier back then. Before Jade had brought up the party.

He took two steps, then stopped. Turning back to his locker, he worked the combination and opened it. Once again he checked to make sure he was alone. He took the condoms out of his pocket, put them in the locker, and shut the door.

Another two steps.

He repeated the action, reopening the locker, checking that he was alone, and putting the condoms in his pocket. The door slammed. He took two steps.

He was going to go insane.

This is not a good idea, he thought. *It makes no sense. Why would Rose want to go to this party? Is Hunter right? Does she really want to see what else is out there? How can she decide something like that when we haven't done much more than kiss?*

"This is nuts!"

"Problem?" a voice said from behind him.

So much for an empty hallway.

Ash turned to find Ms. Barrett standing behind him. "Where did you come from?"

"Initially, a small town in Indiana," she replied. "But I managed to escape right after high school."

Ash was too confused to laugh.

"I mean . . . I didn't hear you sneak up behind me."

"Must be my catlike reflexes," she said. "I think Rose is waiting for you in the student council office."

"I was just on my way there," Ash said.

"Mind if I ask what's going on?" Ms. Barrett asked.

"Nothing," he replied. "Just . . . something."

"That makes it much more clear."

"It's nothing, really," he insisted, more to himself than to the teacher. "Nothing."

"Is it maybe nothing that you should be talking to Rose about?"

"No . . . yes . . . I mean . . . maybe?"

"Well, as long as you're sure."

Ash checked the clock on the wall. It was already after three. If he and Rose were going to get to Gin's, they had to leave right now. "I didn't realize it was so late," he said as he started down the hall. "Have a nice weekend."

"You too!" She called after him. "Be safe!"

What an odd thing to say, he thought as he hurried to the student council office to get Rose. Ms. Barrett didn't usually offer silly phrases like "Be safe" or "Think first" or "Make good choices." She was always saying how teachers were being condescending to students when they talked like that. If was an odd thing to wish him, unless . . .

Rose told her.

But Rose wouldn't have told Ms. Barrett about the thing at Gin's. She hardly even talked about it with me. She wouldn't discuss it with a teacher. Ms. Barrett probably would have been required to stop it if she knew about the party. She certainly wouldn't have limited her response to a simple "Be safe."

Would she?

Ash reached the student council office and stopped. The door was right in front of him, but he couldn't bring himself to open it.

If Rose told Ms. Barrett about the party, maybe that meant she didn't want to go. But Rose was the one that told Jade we were going in the first place.

It was bad enough that Ash was going to make them late. If he brought up his concerns about the party now, she might get upset with him. He did have all day to mention it. In fact, Gin had told Rose about it a couple days ago. He had all that time to say something and he didn't bother.

How can I do it now?

If he tried to stop her from going, she might get upset. Then she might break up with him. No. His only hope was that they'd go to the party and she wouldn't have a good time. Then, she'd stay with him. She'd have to, because . . . well, who else would she go out with?

As he opened the door, he tried to come to terms with the fact that he was an idiot.

"We're late," Rose said as she threw her book into her bag and got up.

"I'm sorry," Ash said, looking apologetic.

Rose hadn't meant it to come out like she was blaming

him. If anything, she was actually hoping he wouldn't show up at all. She had assumed that he had changed his mind. But when the door opened, all hope disappeared.

"Gin doesn't live far, does she?" Ash asked.

"No. It's okay," Rose said. "I'm a bit . . . never mind."

Ash looked at her like he wanted to ask "a bit what?" But he didn't say anything.

She was hoping he would ask something. She was hoping he would say anything.

He didn't.

They kind of just looked at each other for a moment, standing in the open doorway.

"Let's go," Ash said as he held the door for her.

"Okay," she said.

They continued, not saying a word as they walked out of the building. The silence was driving Rose crazy. She wanted him to say something. She wanted him to say, "Let's go home."

All the time they spent together they were never at a loss for words. Sure, they had quiet moments where they simply enjoyed each other's company. But this was different. If Ash started babbling like he did earlier, it might just push Rose over the edge.

"Did you and Ms. Barrett . . ."

Rose waited for Ash to finish his question. She waited for half a block. "Did we what?" she finally asked.

"Nothing," Ash said. "I ran into her on my way to pick you up."

Did she say anything?

"This should be fun," Rose said, attempting damage control. She had made her decision. It was too late to turn back now. She couldn't do that to Ash.

"Yeah," Ash said. He sounded more like they were on their way to get their wisdom teeth extracted than go to a party.

He's probably nervous too.

"So where did you go after school?" Rose asked, searching for a subject they could talk about.

"Just had something to do," he replied. "Nothing big."

She wondered if he had gone to get her a present. That would explain why he didn't want to talk about it. She hoped that wasn't the case. Every time she bought him something, she worried that he might feel he had to return the gesture. She couldn't help herself. She just loved getting him stuff. "Do you like the key chain?" she asked.

"Love it," he said, not looking at her.

"I know I give you a lot of gifts. . . ."

"And I love them all."

"But if it's too much?"

"No," he said, stopping. They were at the corner of Walnut and Magnolia. Only two more blocks to Gin's house. "Why would you think that?"

"I don't want you to feel like you have to buy me stuff."

"I like buying you stuff."

"But you don't *have* to," she insisted. "I mean . . . should I stop buying you so many things?"

"Look, I like your gifts," he said. "But it does get a little expensive."

"I thought so."

"It doesn't mean you have to stop," he said. "But maybe we should slow down. Stick with little things."

"Okay," she said. She was glad they got that out in the open. Maybe Ms. Barrett was right. They *should* talk about the party. "Do—"

"The key chain is a perfect example," Ash added excitedly. "It's cool, with my name and all, and it didn't cost too much money. Look, I'm already using it."

Ash went into his pocket and pulled out the key chain to show her. But it wasn't the only thing that came out. A small red box got hooked on the key chain and landed on the ground. Rose went to pick it up, but stopped herself. "Oh," she said.

They both stood on the street corner, staring at the pack of condoms.

Rose started laughing. She knew it was nervous laughter, but it felt like such a relief. It felt even better when Ash joined in. Before long, they were laughing hysterically, though she suspected neither one of them was exactly sure why.

It felt good. It felt like they were finally on the same page.

"Does lipstick even work on condoms?" she asked when she was finally able to catch her breath.

"Good question," he said.

"It would be kind of counterproductive to the party idea if it didn't," she added cautiously.

"I assumed everyone would bring condoms. Well, if Gin has a problem with me using them, we can just leave," he said.

"Can we?" she asked eagerly.

"Absolutely," he said as he bent to get the condoms off the pavement. He stayed down on his knee for a moment, looking up at her with the oddest expression on his face.

"What's wrong?"

"Nothing," he said, but still didn't move.

"Ash—"

"I love you!"

Ash was so cute. Okay, it was a little weird that he was in the whole marriage proposal kneeling pose with a pack of condoms in his hand instead of an engagement ring, but . . .

"I love you too," she said.

"No," he said as he rose to his feet and slipped the condoms in his pocket. "I *love* you. I'm *in love* with you."

Once again, Rose was speechless.

"I know we've said we love each other before," Ash admitted. "But this is different. I love you. I want to spend the rest of my life with you. I know a billion things can happen to us between now and . . . whenever. But right now, I want you to know that . . . I. Love. You."

Stunned.

That was the only word to describe it. Sure, Rose dreamed of Ash saying these things to her and truly meaning it. He had come close on many occasions. He *had* said that he loved her before. But this collection of words . . . strung together in this way . . .

Stunned.

"I love you," he whispered, and then pulled her into his arms and gave her a kiss unlike any he had given her before.

"We are *not* going to the party," he said as they separated. "I'm sorry if you want to go. But I'm not sharing you with anyone. Not today. Not ever."

"Good," she said. "I didn't really want to go."

"But you were the one that told Jade—"

"I thought I was doing it for you," she explained. "I know. It's stupid."

"Yeah. It is," Ash said with a wink.

"Look, here's the truth," Rose said. "I'm not ready . . . for any of it. Sex or oral sex or whatever everyone's in such a rush to do. I'm just not ready. Not yet . . . and probably not for a while. I'm not saying we have to wait until we're married, but it's not going to be anytime soon. I hope you're okay with that."

"I am."

"I don't know why I thought I was ready. Maybe I hit my head when I slammed into that locker."

"I was the one that slammed into the locker," Ash said.

"See what I mean?" She smiled.

Rose loved being with someone she could be silly and honest with.

And apparently he loved her too.

3:02

Rusty went up and blocked the shot. He was getting better. In fact, it was the best game of Rusty's life. He wasn't sure if it was all the practicing he'd been doing lately or the fact that he had an audience.

Usually he sucked when he knew girls were watching. Or *anyone* was watching, for that matter. Then again, since he didn't know this girl at all, it wasn't like she was going to be criticizing him later.

Rusty took the ball out and drove down the lane, barreling past Brick and up for a shot.

"Two!" he yelled as the ball went *swish.*

"You are on fire!" Brick said with a mixture of shock and awe. "Did someone spike your Propel?"

"Just needed the proper motivation," Rusty said with a nod toward the bleachers.

"We should invite her to all our games."

"Give me time."

"No time like the present," Brick said as he stopped the game.

"No, I meant give me a time-out," Rusty said, covering for his immediate loss of bravado. "I need a drink."

Rusty used dehydration as a distraction. He really wanted to go back and ask the girl out . . . or at least find out her name. There was something about her that was different from the other girls at school. Maybe because she had actually expressed interest in him.

"Check out the time while you're there," Brick yelled.

He grabbed his Propel and chugged the rest of it, tipping back his head and striking a pose for the girl. She was watching again. He looked like a model in one of the TV ads for sports drinks.

I'd go out with me. Why doesn't anyone else want to?

Once he polished off the Propel, Rusty stepped back, jumped, and threw it into the trash, scoring another imaginary 2. Once he confirmed that she had seen that, too, he pawed through Brick's bag, finding his watch. "Oh shit!" he said. "It's after three. We're late."

Brick booked across the court. "What do you mean we're late?"

"Check it out," Rusty held up the watch.

"Oh shit!" Brick said . . . loudly.

Rusty looked over and saw the girl was still watching

them. She must have been impressed by their sparkling vocabulary.

"Let's go," Brick said.

Rusty threw another look over to the bleachers. The girl in the bikini was no longer watching him. She was leaning back with her eyes closed, soaking up the sun. If possible, she looked even hotter than before. If Rusty left now, he may never have another shot at her.

It was also a good excuse not to go to the party, where he'd have to be so . . . exposed in front of everyone.

"Or we could hang here a few more minutes," Brick said.

"We could," Rusty said. He wanted to stay, but he wanted to go, too.

"Go on," Brick pushed. "Show her some of those famous moves."

What moves?

"Look, Brick," Rusty started. He wanted to tell his friend that he had no idea what he was doing. He wanted to say that it was all just stories. He wanted to say that he hardly had any more experience than Brick.

He didn't say any off it.

"I don't work in front of an audience" is what Rusty finally said.

"I'll turn around," Brick added dryly.

"We're really going to be late," Rusty said.

"Wuss."

"Brick," Rusty said with a condescending tone, "do you

think I really want to pass up a sure thing for a chance at some girl whose name I don't know?"

He walked over to his bike without bothering to see if Brick was following. He didn't know how he managed to pull it off, looking so cool, but he did. The reputation would live on . . . at least for the next few minutes.

Rusty couldn't believe himself. The girl was right there literally lying out in front of him. She was interested, too. He could tell. Why else would she keep looking over? And she did flirt with him. Didn't she?

Yet, here he was, hopping on his bike to run away from her. For all the bullshit he could muster in the locker room, he was nothing but a pussy when it came to real life.

Brick tried to balance his basketball in his lap as he rode his bike, trying to keep up with Rusty. He didn't know why he was so stressed about Rusty getting ahead of him. Brick didn't know where Gin lived. If Rusty lost him, then he had the perfect excuse not to go to the party . . . and it wouldn't be an excuse, even.

It was odd how the closer he got to the party becoming reality, the less he minded the virgin jokes.

Unfortunately, Rusty slowed down to let Brick catch up. They took Chestnut down four blocks, speeding past neatly trimmed lawns, minivans, and an angry-looking mailman Rusty nearly plowed down on the sidewalk.

Sweat was pouring off Brick's body as he pedaled after his friend. He was pissed that he hadn't paid more attention to the time. The plan was to hit the showers before they left. Coach always left the shower room open while the baseball team had practice. It was his way to encourage the other teams to get in some unofficial practice of their own.

Considering the locker room was left unattended, the only thing it usually inspired was some heavy making out between the guys and whatever girls they could convince to meet them there. Brick had never even considered trying to get a girl in there. There was something tacky about doing it in the locker room. And really, what kind of girl would find *that* the perfect place to be romantic?

Not that Brick had any belief that the kids that fooled around in the locker room were going there for *romance.*

With no shower, Brick knew he stunk. Sweat mixed with the blacktop, mixed with fear. It was a pungent aroma that this little bike ride was not helping any.

"Rusty!"

"What!"

Rusty turned left on Sycamore and pedaled even faster.

Brick wanted to say they should have showered. He wanted to suggest stopping off at his place for a few minutes. He wanted to tell Rusty to forget the whole thing.

He said none of that stuff.

Rusty turned left on Walnut. It seemed to Brick that they were going back the way they had come, but he didn't say anything. Rusty knew where they were going and he pedaled there like a man on a mission.

Brick finally managed to catch up to his friend at the corner of Walnut and Maple. They pedaled together for a moment before Brick turned right and Rusty broke left.

"Hey!" Rusty yelled as he swung around. "Where you going?"

"I figured she lives this way," Brick said as he braked.

"Why'd you figure that?"

"The other way takes us back to school," Brick said, while having a crazy thought. "You *do* know where Gin lives, don't you?"

The fact that Rusty didn't answer right away was all the confirmation Brick needed.

"I was hoping *you* did," Rusty finally said.

Brick was torn between anger and extreme relief. Actually he was leaning far more toward the relief side, but he couldn't let that show.

"How the hell would I know where she lives?" Brick asked. "I was never with her."

"Hey, we did it in the locker room," Rusty said defensively. "It's not like I walked her home afterwards."

"Yeah, why would you do that?" Brick said sarcastically. "Okay, we can figure this out. What direction does she usually walk when she leaves school?"

"You planning on going door to door asking if this is the place with the blowjob party?" Rusty asked.

"Big talk for a moron who can't even think to ask for an address," Brick replied. This "angry act" was getting out of hand. He wasn't even the least bit upset. He was going to start reining it in, when something caught his eye.

Looking a couple blocks down Walnut, Brick saw Rose and Ash walking hand in hand. They appeared to be walking to Ash's house. He lived back toward school.

Brick had been to *that* house before.

He thought Rose and Ash were supposed to be going to the party. At least, that's what Hunter had said earlier. But Brick was pretty sure that Gin's house had to be in the opposite direction. The way they were holding hands and leaning in together, it was possible Rose and Ash had changed their minds about going. Either way, it would only take a moment to shoot down the street and either join up with them or ask directions to Gin's.

Brick looked at Rusty. It would have been so easy to point out their friends and go after them. Yet those weren't the words that came out of his mouth.

"Race you back to the court," he said. "If I get there first, I'm asking your new girlfriend out."

While Rusty considered the offer, Brick hoped that he didn't notice Rose and Ash down the street. Rusty's head did turn in that direction, but he didn't react like he had seen them.

"Deal," Rusty said as he took off on his bike.

"Asshole!" Brick shouted as he hurried after his friend.

He was surprised by the amount of relief he felt over not having to go to the party.

Thank God Gin didn't make up invitations.

3:03

Hunter finished zipping up as he came down the stairs. It was like he was pissing every fifteen minutes lately. He'd hardly even had anything to drink all day, but he was constantly running to the john. It wasn't the frequency that was bothering him the most, though. It was the burning sensation. That was new, and definitely not fun.

"What are you doing?" Perry asked as Hunter came into the living room.

"Hmm?" Hunter asked, throwing an innocent look on his face. That same look would help him get away with murder, as far as his parents were concerned.

"Why is there a green condom hanging out of your mouth?"

Hunter smiled. He knew he had to look hysterical. He took a deep breath and blew, inflating the green condom way past magnum size. He took it out of his mouth and tied off the end.

"Party balloons," he said as he smacked the condom across the room and watched as it floated to Perry. It looked just like a regular balloon, except for the reservoir tip.

"There's money well spent," Perry said. He hit the condom when it came to him and sent it back across his living room to Hunter.

"Back atch'ya,'" Hunter said as he slammed it back.

Perry returned the serve as they got into a game of Living Room Condom-Balloon Volleyball using the couch as their net.

Hunter couldn't help but notice that Perry kept looking at the grandfather clock in the corner.

"Will you cool it," Hunter said as he lobbed a high one back at Perry. "The party's not going to start without me."

"I didn't know this was the kind of thing you could be fashionably late to," Perry said as he bounced the condom back.

"I can be whatever I want," Hunter said. "Let me teach you a few things about girls."

"Oh yes . . . this should be enlightening."

"Girls play hard to get," Hunter said. "They make this whole sex thing into a game."

"Yet we're the ones playing with a condom full of your hot air," Perry said.

"Are you listening or are you bitching?"

"I can do both."

Hunter knew that was true. Years of experience had proven that.

"Continue," Perry added.

"We have to make it a bigger game," Hunter said. "They play hard to get. We play harder."

"No pun intended," Perry said.

"I've got Gin so wrapped around my dick that she's usually begging for it," Hunter said. It was true. He'd been with girls in their school . . . many, many, girls . . . but none of them were willing to do the things that Gin was willing to do with him. He sometimes considered trying out a few things with Perry, but you just don't do those kinds of things to a friend.

"Should I be taking notes?" Perry asked.

"Why do you have to be such an ass?" Hunter grabbed the condom balloon and jumped over the back of the couch, falling into the seat. "I'm trying to help you out here."

"Telling me to play hard to get isn't exactly news," Perry said as he sat down. "It's one of those things that have been going around for generations. And don't tell me you've *ever* played hard to get. You're pretty damn easy to get, as far as I can tell."

"Well, maybe it's an 'I'm out of your league' thing," Hunter said, reconsidering his own advice. "Act like you can have any girl and *every* girl will want you. Just look at my track record."

"So treat girls like shit and you can have your way with them?"

"It's amazing the things girls will let you get away with," Hunter explained. "They want it just as bad as us guys. But they're all trained to act like they're supposed to stay virgins until they get married. You act like it's their loss . . . like they're the ones missing out. They'll come knocking on your door."

"I thought most guys relied on begging," Perry said.

"Losers like Rod do," Hunter said. "Sure, begging probably works, but why put the girl in the power position. I mean, Gin—"

"You know, Gin really works in every scenario you come up with, doesn't she?"

"Can I help it if the girl's got no morals?" Hunter laughed. "I mean, she *really* does anything I tell her. I'll let you in on a secret. This party . . . she did see it on some TV show and told me about it. It took me a whole afternoon to convince her what a great thing it was. Now she acts like it was entirely her idea. And I let her because no one would go if they knew I was the one behind it. See, it's all how you play it."

"And it probably helps that she's the most gullible girl on the face of the earth."

"Doesn't hurt," Hunter said. "Do you know *why* she thinks the party's a great idea? She thinks she's going to be the one in control. She's the one putting the party together. She picked the people to come. She gets to tell everyone what to do. She's the one who has us by the balls—"

"Literally."

"But she's the one that's going to end up with a mouthful of *me*," Hunter said, and smiled. "Am I good or what?"

"Yet, she still managed to get you to go down on her."

"Just once," Hunter said, picking up a blue condom and tearing the packet open with his teeth. "Here. Help me blow these up."

Perry took the blue condom from Hunter and looked it over. It smelled like blueberries. Probably tasted like blueberries too, but Perry wasn't about to find out. There were *some* things he had no intention of putting in his mouth. He watched as Hunter pulled out an orange condom and began to blow air into it.

They'd had plenty of these conversations over the course of their friendship where Hunter would extol the virtues about being . . . well, Hunter. It was during these times that Perry understood Vi's feeling that Hunter wasn't a good friend. But she never saw the real Hunter. The one that wasn't all bluster and bravado. That Hunter was nowhere around today. The Hunter that Perry was spending the day with was Horny Hunter. And not the good Horny Hunter that was fun to be around. This was the annoying asshole Horny Hunter who was God's gift to the world.

"Are you going to blow?" Horny Hunter asked as he tied off another condom balloon.

Oh, the things going through Perry's mind in response to *that* question.

He didn't say any of them. Instead, he lifted the blueberry condom to his lips and slowly filled it with air. It didn't actually taste that bad. He'd had far worse things in his mouth before.

Perry watched Hunter as he blew. It was possible that Vi was right all those times she ranted about Hunter. He might be a total jerk. Perry could be making excuses for Hunter and defending him for reasons his friend didn't deserve. But Hunter always treated him well. There was only one area of their friendship where Hunter never reciprocated. Perry couldn't blame him for not wanting to. Most guys didn't want to.

As Perry tied off the blue balloon, he wondered for the million-and-first time why he wasn't like most guys.

"Here." Perry bounced the condom balloon over to Hunter.

"Good job," Hunter said, handing Perry a purple condom. It smelled—not surprisingly—like grape. "A little more air this time."

A little more air this time.

Perry couldn't even blow up a damn balloon without Hunter telling him how to do it better. Like Hunter had all the answers.

Where did that *come from?*

Perry didn't usually get pissed at Hunter. Sure, there were times when Hunter would upset him . . . when Hunter made him sad. But the brief flash of anger he just had was unprecedented. Perry didn't get mad. He got sarcastic.

"This is going to be so great," Hunter said once again.

"Uh-huh," Perry said, only because he knew Hunter was waiting for a comment.

"Dude, you *so* owe me one."

Perry couldn't take it anymore, he totally lost it. "What do I owe you for?" he raged. "What the hell do I owe you for!"

Hunter was speechless, which was just about as unheard of as Perry getting angry.

"You got me invited to some stupid party . . . a party you already told me Gin didn't even want me at. Why? Am I some fucking leper?"

"Dude, chill."

"No, dude. I will not *chill,*" Perry said, his anger building. "You never even asked me if I wanted to go to the party."

"Of course you want—"

"Do you understand that Vi's going to be there?" Perry steamed. "I've only known her since I was *born.* Do you think I want to make her go—"

"No one's making her do anything," Hunter said. "What the hell is wrong with you? You're not *forcing* Vi to do anything."

"Right," Perry said. " 'Cause you're the expert on forcing friends to do things that they don't want to do."

"What the fuck is wrong with you?"

Damned if I know, Perry thought. The one thing he knew

for certain was that this argument had nothing to do with Vi. He figured the two of them would just take a pass when it came time to be together. It wasn't even a question. That's why he never even brought it up to her.

No, this argument . . . this *fight* wasn't about Vi.

"I've never made you do anything you didn't want to do," Hunter said.

That was true too. That was also Perry's problem. He let Hunter treat him that way because he liked it.

I am one sick fuck.

"I'm not going to the party," Perry said.

"Fine," Hunter said, collecting his condom balloons. "More action for me."

Perry seethed as he watched Hunter leave his house without another word.

He didn't know what he expected to happen. He didn't know why he even had the outburst in the first place. The one thing he didn't think would happen would be that Hunter would just up and leave without another word. He didn't even try to convince Perry that he should go.

Perry rushed to the front window and watched as Hunter crossed the lawn and hit the sidewalk. He wasn't even moving at an angry pace. He was taking a leisurely stroll as if his best friend hadn't just reamed him out for no apparent reason.

That burned Perry more than anything.

Perry knew that he had feelings for Hunter that would never be returned. He even accepted the fact that it was his problem and not Hunter's fault. But for Hunter to hardly even acknowledge their *friendship*—that was too much.

As Hunter moved out of eyesight, Perry closed the curtains. The couch was too far away. He just sat on the floor. He was glad that he let Hunter know his feelings. He just wished that he had been more coherent. He had rehearsed similar conversations in his mind on numerous occasions, knowing it would never come out the way he had intended it.

Boy, did I get that part right.

Perry still couldn't believe that Hunter just left. He wasn't sure why it surprised him. They'd had plenty of fights over the years and Hunter always ended them by leaving. Hunter didn't like confrontation.

But this was different. This wasn't a stupid fight over Xbox. This was real.

Perry closed his eyes, trying to calm himself. His mom was always preaching the benefits of yoga and meditation. It all seemed a little too *gay* for Perry, which was saying something. Now he wished he knew some techniques.

He tried to let the anger wash out of him, but it was still there. Behind all that anger was a hint of fear, too. Hunter wasn't used to being attacked like that. No one ever *dared* speak up against Hunter Kennedy.

The fear was brief, however. There was no real concern as far as, say, losing Hunter's friendship. If there was one thing Perry knew better than anyone, it was that Hunter would come back.

Hunter always came back.

3:04

Skye stared at the Wiggles alarm clock by Vicki's bed. Rod was sitting beside her doing the same thing.

On average, it took her mom a half hour to get home from work. That was during rush hour. If she hit all green lights she might make it in twenty to twenty-five minutes. But if she was speeding, there was no telling how fast she could get there.

Skye couldn't worry about that anymore. She'd find out how angry her mom was soon enough. There was something else bothering her at the moment.

"Rod?"

He seemed surprised that she was speaking to him. "Yes?"

"How come we never . . . did what we just did before?"

"Got caught?"

"No," she said. She wasn't sure if he was making a lame joke or was actually being lame. "Before we got caught."

"You never asked," he replied without even bothering to act like he was thinking it over.

"But you never had to ask me," she replied. "I just gave it to you."

"Yeah, but that's different."

"How?"

"It just is," Rod said, as if that explained everything. "Look, no guy's going to do that without being asked to. And even then . . . it just doesn't happen."

"Oh," she said, as if it made perfect sense. The only thing she really understood was that she didn't understand Rod at all.

"We should go," Rod said. "We're going to be late."

"Haven't you been paying attention?" Skye asked. "My mom will be home any minute. She's going to kill me. I can't go anywhere."

"Your mom just said she was coming home. She never said you had to stay here," Rod said. "I doubt you can get in any more trouble than you're already in. Why not just postpone it an hour and have some fun first? It could be the last time you have fun for a while."

Needless to say, it was a tempting offer. She wished she could put her mom off forever. But that wouldn't really make the situation any better.

"We have to wait for Vi," Skye reminded him. Like she

could care about Vi at the moment. She wasn't about to leave the house and piss her mom off anymore.

"Can't she just meet us on the way?"

"If she had a cell phone," Skye said. "But since we can't call her, how's she going to know?"

"Mark can tell her we left when she gets here."

"Because Mark is really going to help us out," Skye said. She was being unfair, really. The moment they heard that Mom was coming home, Mark had stopped laying into her and let them go to her room to wait. "If I leave the house, Mom will blame him."

"Good, let her take out her anger on him and then calm down by the time you get back."

"You just don't understand how this works," Skye said. Her mom wasn't going to be calm for a very, very, long time.

They had had "the talk" over two years ago. Skye had assured her mom she wasn't anywhere near ready to have sex. At the time, it was true. They even made an agreement like she had seen on *The Dr. Donovan Show.* She promised her mom that she'd come to talk about it more when she felt she was ready. They would discuss the decision and all the ramifications together so that Skye could really be prepared for what she was getting into.

But that was the last thing they had ever said on the subject.

The problem was that they'd had "the talk" before she met Rod. She made that stupid promise before she and Rod spent the summer together . . . before that perfect night with the thunderstorm. Before she had sex with a boy she was still not sure she even loved.

It wasn't like she was going to stop in the middle of their clothes coming off to call her mom and discuss the ramifications of what was going to happen. She wasn't exactly thinking about any "pact" in the moment. She wasn't really thinking at all. Maybe if she had been thinking, she wouldn't be minutes away from what would probably be the most intense grounding ever seen in history.

It wasn't just the fact that she was sleeping with Rod that was the problem. Skye had broken her agreement and had been lying to her mother ever since the first time she was with him. The worst part was how surprisingly easy it was for her to do.

Her mom had done everything right as far as Dr. Donovan would have been concerned. Okay, maybe her mom should have brought up the subject once or twice since their talk—especially since Skye was seeing Rod. But that defense wasn't going to win her any points now. Perhaps her mom didn't want to know what was going on.

"Maybe I should go," Rod said.

Skye wasn't sure if he meant he should go to the party, or just go so he wasn't there when Mom got home. She hoped that he wasn't actually suggesting that he'd go to the party without her.

"Stop looking at the clock!" Skye yelled.

"Sorry," he mumbled.

Skye couldn't believe that she was about to get in the biggest trouble of her life and that her *loving* boyfriend was only worried about missing a group-sex party.

"I don't know if we're going to be able to hang out much over the next couple weeks . . . or months," Skye said, preparing him for the worst.

"We'll see each other in school," Rod said.

That wasn't helping. What could they do in school? It was the hours after school when she was stuck at home, cut off from the world, that Skye was worried about. She couldn't imagine Rod was going to be faithful for the entire time she was punished.

If the rumors were true, she wasn't sure that he was being faithful to her now.

"You know, your mom doesn't really know anything," Rod said. "We could tell her Vicki was making it up. Or she was confused. She *is* only five."

Skye had never believed any of the rumors about Rod. It was easy to blow it off as girls like Gin spreading stuff because they were jealous. But if Skye never really believed it, why was she even considering going to this Rainbow Party thing in the first place? Was she so afraid of losing him that she was doing it just to make him happy? Or was she just afraid of losing the fact that she had *someone*?

She thought of Vi. Her best friend seemed to have it all: loving parents, great friends. But all she did was complain about the one thing she didn't have: a boyfriend. Skye wasn't so sure that was something worth complaining about. At the same time, she was afraid of suddenly finding herself without a guy as well.

Maybe this was why she never really asked herself these questions. She was afraid that she didn't have any answers.

"Yeah," Rod continued. "Vicki's only five. We could act like we didn't know what she was talking about. Maybe Mark would even go along. He seemed to calm down once he knew your mom was coming home and he'd be off the hook."

Skye finally realized why she wanted to go to the party. She wanted Rod to see her with other guys. She wanted him to know that she could get whomever she wanted. She wanted him to know what he had.

Then again, maybe she just wanted to show *herself* what she could get.

That was when she finally made a decision. She wished she could have been more surprised about it.

"Maybe you *should* go," she said, but she wasn't just talking about the party.

"You mean it?" he asked.

A small part of her had been hoping to get an argument that he wanted to stay with her. Something to suggest that he truly cared about her as much as he kept saying he did. The fact that he tried to cover the excitement in his voice didn't make it hurt any less.

"No reason we should both get yelled at," Skye said as she slowly got off the bed. "Come on, I'll go downstairs with you."

"Yeah," Rod said. "Your mom will probably be more pissed if I'm still here when she gets home."

Skye knew he was right. She also knew that she deserved a guy that didn't care how much trouble he was going to be in, so long as he was there for her. One good thing about the punishment she was about to get; it would keep her from having to go to this dumb-ass party. The kind of guy she was looking for was definitely not going to be there.

Syke and Rod walked downstairs together. His silence told her more than anything he had ever said to her.

"Where are you going?" Skye's brother asked as they came down the stairs. "Mom isn't going to like it if you're not here when she gets home."

"I'm just saying good-bye to Rod," Skye said as they moved into the living room.

"That's brave," Mark said to Rod. "Leaving Skye here to catch hell on her own."

Rod knew he was in a lose-lose situation. "I figured you wanted me to leave. I thought you hated me."

"Oh, I do hate you," Mark said. "But now I don't respect you either."

Rod didn't know what to do. He wanted to stay. He wanted to be there for Skye, but what good would it do? He'd probably just make Mrs. Nicholas angrier.

He had only seen her really angry one time. A couple months back, he and Skye were supposed to be watching Vicki. Somehow she managed to get out of the house and down to the playground without either of them noticing she was gone.

Mrs. Nicholas was pissed beyond belief that day.

Somehow, Rod suspected today was going to be worse.

No. It was for the best that he was leaving. Skye would calm her mother down. She'd be punished, but eventually they'd be allowed to see each other again. In the meantime, it wouldn't hurt to have a break. Things were getting a little too serious than he had liked with Skye, anyway.

"Are you going home?" Vicki asked. She sounding disappointed. Rod knew she had a little crush on him. It was cute.

"Yeah, Vicki," he said. "I have to go somewhere."

Skye shot a look at him, but didn't say anything.

"Will you come over tomorrow?" Vicki asked.

"We'll have to see about that," Rod said.

"Well, don't let my sister's problems bother you in the least," Mark said as he walked into the foyer and opened the front door. "I'm sure she'll get along fine without you. Have a great day."

Mark made no sense whatsoever, Rod thought. A few minutes ago, he was ready to kill Rod, and now he didn't want him to leave. Rod was glad he was an only child.

"I'm gonna take off," Rod said to Skye.

"You know . . . maybe that's a good idea," Mark agreed, still holding the door.

Rod went in to kiss Skye, but she pulled away. He didn't know why. None of this was *his* fault. She was the one who had wanted to go up to her mom's room. She was the one that had started it.

It wasn't like they were even having sex. He could have totally kept his clothes on for what they were doing. It was such a waste to get into trouble over nothing.

"I love you," he whispered.

"Whatever," Skye said.

The sound of tires screeching in the driveway came through the open door.

A car door slammed.

Footsteps.

"Skye!"

Mark stepped away from the front door as their mom came in. She looked far more pissed than she had on that day they had lost Vicki.

"Mommy?" Vicki asked, unaware of what she was standing in the middle of.

"Hi honey," she replied with a tight smile.

Skye's mom came into the room and pulled her youngest child up in a hug.

"I think maybe Mark wants to take you to the playground," she said.

"I don't have my shoes." Vicki pointed to her bare feet.

"Mark can put them on for you."

"He ties them too tight," Vicki said.

"Fine," Mrs. Nicholas said. "Are they in your room?"

Vicki nodded her head.

Mrs. Nicholas took Vicki by the hand. "Let's go put them on." Then she turned to Skye. "You stay right here." Then to Rod. "You'd better be gone when I get back."

"Yes ma'am," Rod said. His trembling voice betrayed the look of relief on his face.

"I better go," Rod said to Skye as her mom went upstairs.

"Ya think?"

"Call me tonight," Rod said as he made his way for the door. "If you can."

"Yeah," Skye said.

He doubted that he was going to hear from her that night. For some reason, he got the feeling that he wasn't going to hear from her for a while.

What a crazy day.

Actually, it was just a crazy afternoon. In the span of a few hours, Vi had actually thought about stealing one best friend's boyfriend and found out she was going to be expected to . . . service . . . another best friend. And she hadn't even *seen* that second best friend all day.

What a crazy day.

Vi's foot made a circle in the sand beneath the swing set

as her hand twisted the charm bracelet. Out of options, she had come to the playground to wait out the start of the party. The playground was almost directly in the middle of the neighborhood between Perry's and Skye's houses.

She had considered going to Perry's, but what would she say?

She had considered going to Skye's, but what was the point?

Three o'clock came and went and she hadn't moved.

The decision was already made that she was going to the party. She would do what she had to do and leave. There really didn't have to be any more to it than that. She might even have fun. Whatever happened between her and Rod was going to stay within the party. She wouldn't even look at him.

Easier said than done.

She still couldn't stop thinking about Rod. It's not like she got chances like this every day. Nobody she knew ever did anything like this. But she couldn't stop thinking about tomorrow. How would she go back to having Rod just be her best friend's boyfriend?

Tomorrow was the real problem. Vi didn't like to think about tomorrow. She knew that things would change. Things would have to change. At the very least, she probably wouldn't be able to look at Rod the same way again. She knew that she wouldn't be able to listen to Skye talk about him anymore. How could she sit and listen to Skye go on about things that Vi had briefly experienced on her own?

Perry was, by far, the easier part to think about. She'd just skip him when that turn in the rotation came around. Perry would probably agree that it was the best thing to do. If anyone said anything, well screw 'em. She was not going to ruin a friendship for a few minutes of . . . pleasure?

Nothing seemed all that *pleasurable* at the moment.

It was such a crazy day.

Parties were supposed to be fun. "Fooling around" was supposed to be fun. That's why it was called "fooling around," after all. But nothing about this was fun.

Vi had already come up with about a hundred excuses why she could skip this afternoon. Each and every one of them totally believable. The funny part was that she never even considered the truth. Simply saying that she wasn't really into it was not an option. Skye would hit her with a bunch of questions. Eventually Vi would slip up and mention Rod.

No. The lies would have been easy. Blaming her parents. Claiming some kind of emergency. Simply saying she lost track of time. Each of them would have worked and been totally believable. But none of them helped with the one thing she was truly afraid of. The one reason more than any other that she really was considering going to the party.

What if Skye went without her?

Vi took a deep breath and got off the swing. She moved off toward Skye's house. She knew she was late. Skye would probably be upset. Vi really didn't care. If Skye had cared about Vi's feelings, then they would have stayed together after school. Instead, Vi got ditched while Skye and Rod got off.

Sometimes Skye could be so thoughtless.

She doesn't deserve a guy like Rod.

"I really have to stop that," she said out loud to herself.

It was a weird thing to both hate and love her best friend at the same time.

As Vi turned onto Birch she saw Rod coming out of Skye's house. Skye wasn't with him. That wasn't a good sign. Maybe Vi was too late and they had gotten into a fight or something.

She caught up with Rod as he hit the sidewalk. He almost went right past her, but she grabbed him by the arm. "Hey," she said. "Where's Skye?"

"Oh," Rod said, like he just realized that she was talking to him. "Inside."

"Is she coming?"

"I don't think so."

Vi looked up at the house. She could see Skye watching them from the living room window. Even at that distance, Vi could tell something was wrong.

"Did you guys have a fight?" she asked.

"Her mom came home."

"No!" Vi looked back at her friend. She didn't know what to do. "Did she catch you?"

"Not exactly," Rod said. "But she knows."

"Oh God." Vi had a pretty good idea what Skye was in for. She knew all about Skye's "agreement." Mrs. Nicholas was usually very calm and understanding. But only to a point.

"Yeah. I got out of there immediately."

"I guess we're not going to the party." She wasn't entirely disappointed. Especially since she knew she wasn't the only one not going to be there.

"Skye told me I could go," Rod smiled.

"She did? She told you that you could go to the party?"

"Yep."

Something was up. That was not the Skye that Vi knew. There was no way Skye would let him go without her.

"So, wait." She needed a clarification. "Skye's mom comes home. She freaks out over the two of you having sex—"

"We weren't having sex."

"Well, whatever you were doing. Fooling around. Skye's mom doesn't like it. She gets angry. Kicks you out of the house. And what? Skye's last words to you are 'Don't skip the party on account of me'?"

"Something like that."

Vi didn't know which was more stupid. The fact that he thought that's how things really went down or the fact that he thought she'd buy it.

"Then again, Vi . . . *Violet* . . . ," Rod said as he put an arm around her. "We could go to my place and have a private party of our own."

And there it was. The offer she had been waiting for. The words she had been dying to hear. Skye and Rod were probably not a couple anymore. Skye's mom would see to that. There's no way in hell she would ever allow that boy under her roof again.

So, if Skye and Rod had effectively broken up . . .

And Skye had supposedly given him permission . . .

And Rod was a guy that had no problem admitting that he loved someone . . .

There was only one thing she could say to that.

"Fuck. Off."

3:05

"Where the hell is everybody?" Gin asked.

Sandy shrugged. She didn't know the answer to that question any more than she did the last three times Gin asked.

"Maybe they're all being fashionably late," Sandy suggested.

"This isn't that kind of party," Gin said.

Sandy was glad she wasn't in charge, because the hostess was *way* stressed. All the work was done. They just had to wait for everyone to arrive. Gin was worrying for no reason, though. People always came late.

Sandy understood how Gin felt. She wanted the party to start too. She wanted to get it over with. If Gin was right, then it probably wasn't going to last long. Sandy could certainly put up with what she was going to have to do for a short time. It wasn't like she was giving up her virginity. Really, it wasn't even sex.

She could do this. If only to get it over with. Then, maybe, she wouldn't have to worry about it anymore. Once she got it out of the way she could focus on what her heart truly wanted.

She couldn't wait for Rusty to get there.

She had no idea how he would feel about her afterward. If she was good, he might come back for more. Then maybe they'd fall in love and *make* love. That'd be cool.

That would be ridiculous.

Sandy was still trying to convince herself that this Rainbow Party was going to be a life-changing experience. And while it might change her life somehow, she was beginning to doubt that the change would be for the better.

Since she didn't like that thought, she tried to put it out of her mind.

"So how does this work?" Sandy asked. "Do we start when the first guy gets here and then everyone joins in as they arrive? Do we wait until everyone is here?"

"Do I *look* like an expert?" Gin demanded.

Sandy had to think about that for a moment. "Well . . . *yes.*"

"Shows what you know," Gin mumbled.

What does that *mean?*

Whenever Sandy got nervous, she couldn't shut up. It drove her crazy, but probably not half as crazy as she was driving Gin. But she still couldn't stop herself. "Who do you think will show first?"

"How the hell should I know?" Gin snapped. "I thought everyone would be here by now."

"I know," Sandy agreed. "If I wasn't already here, I'd be here now."

"That's some logic you use there."

"I think it will be Hunter," Sandy said. "Since he's the closest to you."

"Oh no," Gin said, trying to sound like it didn't matter. "Hunter will not be the first to arrive. He's probably waiting at Perry's until the last possible second. He likes to make an entrance."

"Well, then—"

"Why do you keep talking?" Gin asked.

"Nervous habit."

"Well, get over it," Gin said. "There's still time to un-invite you."

Oh please. Could you?

"I don't know why you even invited me in the first place," Sandy said. "And don't say 'Sandra Dee.' I know that's not the reason."

Gin put her hand on Sandy's shoulder. "You're my best friend. Why wouldn't I invite you?"

For a moment, Sandy actually believed her. There was something in Gin's eyes that implied she was being honest. It was something that Sandy had never seen before. But just because Sandy had never seen it before didn't mean it was true. Besides, she had a point to make.

"Because you know this isn't my thing," she said. "You know I've never done anything even close to this before. You know it scares the hell out of me."

There. She said it. And yet, she didn't feel any better.

"But you came," Gin reminded her. "So maybe it *is* 'your thing.' Maybe you were just waiting for the right time to let yourself go and have some real fun."

"And you just happen to know what's best for me?"

"What can I say? Call it a gift." Gin sat down on the green suede couch.

But that wasn't it. Sandy was beginning to suspect that Gin's motives weren't all that friendly. "You don't think I'll go through with it. You think I'll chicken out."

"I never said that."

"This whole afternoon is about getting what you want. Instant popularity, because you were the only one in school with the guts to pull this kind of thing off." Sandy was amazed by the bizarre manipulation of it all. "And once you're popular, you won't need me as a best friend anymore. So when I go running out of here like the baby you keep telling me I am, you'll have a reason to stop being my friend."

Sandy couldn't believe how much sense that craziness made. It was totally Gin's way of thinking. Sandy wondered—not for the first time—what had made Gin such a cynical . . .

you know, the "b" word. Gin had a great life and wonderful parents who gave her anything she asked for. Yet she filled her afternoons with guys she didn't care about and orchestrated grand schemes to take down people. Like she knew what was best for everyone . . . except herself.

Well, Sandy wasn't about to fall for one of Gin's plans. If Gin was so sure Sandy would bail, Sandy would simply prove that Gin didn't know everything. Sandy was going to go through with it, whether she wanted to or not.

"Believe what you want to believe," Gin said, hoping to put an end to the argument. "But you have no idea what you're talking about."

"I'm here to stay," Sandy said. She didn't look too happy about her decision.

Sandy couldn't have been further from the truth if she tried. Gin wasn't often nice to people for no reason. And if this was the kind of response she got, she doubted she'd be doing it too often.

She got up from the couch, needing to move. She went straight for the window.

Gin was ready to kill. The intense anger she felt was covering up something else entirely, but she didn't like to think about *that.* Instead, she directed her anger at every single person who was late. She imagined killing them all in escalating degrees of violence, depending on how late they arrived. Unfortunately, the innocent bystander of her rage was Sandy simply because she was the only one actually in the room.

"See anyone yet?" Sandy asked.

"No." Gin pulled the curtains shut. It wasn't like looking out the window was going to make them get there any faster. It also would have looked pathetic if Jade or Skye caught her.

I hope they're not the first to show.

It had to be a boy. It would be great if it was Hunter. She'd even take Brick or Rusty. But if any of the girls showed up first and they had to wait around for the boys . . .

It would have made more sense for the boys to show up first. Hell, Gin expected them to be beating down the door to get in. It's not like they had a bunch of girls ready, willing, and on their knees every day.

Where are they?

"Should we start the music?" Sandy asked.

"No," Gin replied. She even had that part planned out. The first guests would arrive to Eminem. Marilyn Manson would get things going. They'd be in full swing by the time she calmed the mood with some Usher. The iPod playlist would wind the party down with a little John Mayer, just to make Sandy happy.

They would run out of songs by four thirty, which would be way more than enough time. Cleanup would only take a few minutes since she had laid out an old blanket on the floor. By the time Gin's parents got home there would be no evidence. She'd even delete the playlist titled RAINBOW PARTY.

"They'll be here," Sandy said. "Just like you planned. Don't worry."

"Of course they're going to be here," Gin said, wanting to peek out the window again. "Why do you think I'm worried?"

"Because you're pacing."

Gin stopped in the middle of the living room. She hadn't realized she had been walking back and forth. This was getting ridiculous. Gin Norris did not behave this way.

"I need a drink," Gin said as she left the room.

"Yeah, let's get some bottled water," Sandy said as she followed.

"That's not what I had in mind." Gin bypassed the kitchen for her dad's study. That's where he kept the hard liquor. They were all sitting out in a row of glass bottles on the cute little sidebar Mom had bought at The Bombay Company.

"Oh, you mean a *drink,* drink," Sandy said, stating the obvious.

Gin grabbed a glass off the bar and looked over the selection. "You want anything?"

"No thanks."

I'm shocked.

She considered going with her namesake, Gin, but she wasn't in that kind of mood. It looked like today was the day for her old friend, Jack. She twisted the lid off the bottle of Jack Daniel's and carefully poured a little in the glass. Her dad rarely paid attention to the exact amount of alcohol in the bottles, since he trusted his only child to never touch the stuff. As long as she didn't drink too much from any one bottle, he'd never know.

The Jack was bitter as it went down her throat. It burned a bit too. She had been having trouble swallowing all day. It felt like she was coming down with a sore throat. Gin hoped it wouldn't affect her performance.

Gin put the glass back down on the sidebar. "I like it," she said.

"The drink?"

"You keep asking dumb questions like I can give you some reason," Gin continued. "Like there's some explanation that will make you understand why I do what I do. Well, that's all there is. *I like it.* I like fooling around with guys. It's fun. It's no different from what Hunter does. But all the guys want to be his friend, while none of the girls want to be mine. And you know what? I don't care. I'm enjoying myself. Does it make me a horrible person? Does it mean that I have something missing from my life? Does it mean that I really hate myself inside?"

"Does it?"

"No, Sandy," Gin said. "It just means I like to have fun."

Gin let that sink in for a moment. She was impressed. She almost had herself believing it too.

"I think someone's here," Sandy said. She had turned her attention to the window during the silence.

Sandy bolted into the hall.

"Wait," Gin commanded. "Don't look too eager. You have to be calm when you open the door."

"Okay."

Gin slowly, *calmly,* led Sandy back through the house, even though she was freaking out a little on the inside.

Maybe they were taking too long, because when they got to the living room they could already hear whoever it was opening the door.

"Ginger!" a voice called out. "Hey honey, it's just me."

Gin froze. She was about to throw up what little Jack she had in her stomach.

"Dad?"

"Fuck!" Sandy whispered. It was the first time Gin had ever heard her swear.

She took the word right out of my mouth.

Gin scanned the living room. There was nothing to indicate a party was supposed to be happening. The blanket looked out of place lying on the floor, but it wasn't a problem.

"There you are," Gin's dad said as he came into the living room carrying a grocery bag. "What, no hug?"

"I'm just surprised," Gin said, realizing that her breath smelled like Jack Daniel's. "You *never* come home early."

"We settled the Cruise case," he replied as he put the bag down on the sofa table. "That was a pleasant little surprise. To celebrate, I figured I'd come home early and hang with my favorite girl. Hi, Sandy."

"Hi."

"How are you?"

"Fine."

Gin's father looked at her oddly. "Okay, then." He looked back at Gin. "I'm still waiting for that hug."

Gin clamped her mouth shut and walked to her father. She gave him a quick hug, then slowly backed away.

"Why's it so dark in here?" he asked as he went to open the curtains.

Please don't let anyone be coming up the walk.

For the first time that afternoon, Gin was hoping *no one* showed up for her party.

"That's better." He turned back to the room away from the window. "What's going on in here? You moved all the furniture back."

"We were going to dance," Gin said, quickly picking up her iPod. "Try out some moves from TRL."

"Well, don't let me interrupt," her dad replied. "I have a few things to go over in my study. But when I'm done we can make dinner together. Surprise your mom. I stopped at the store to pick up a few things. Of course, Sandy, you're welcome to stay."

"Thanks."

Gin suddenly freaked. She wasn't sure if she had put the cap back on the bottle of Jack. She *was* sure that the glass she drank out of was still sitting out on the bar.

As she tried to figure out a distraction, she looked out the window and saw there was a much bigger problem coming up the walk. She was allowed to have Sandy over when her parents weren't home. Girls were perfectly fine to have in the house. But boys were a definite no.

And here was one about to ring the doorbell.

But she could explain that, too. Hunter was smart enough to play along if she told him he couldn't come in. Her dad was between her and the door, though. If he answered it, Hunter was also smart enough to figure the party was busted and would go on his way.

Everything was fine.

Except for the fact that Hunter was carrying a bunch of balloons with him. That would be harder to explain. Why would a boy be bringing her balloons?

Oh shit! They're not *balloons.*

Over the Rainbow

7:35

Gin took one last look in her compact makeup mirror. She had nervously chewed off most of her lipstick on the way to school. That would not do at all.

She reached into her purse and pulled out her tube of Harlot. The name was so much more fitting now than when she had bought it three weeks ago. She applied the color to her lips as the daylight faded around her. It didn't look half as good as she had thought it was going to. But it was all she had on her at the moment.

Gin tried to ignore the stares as well-dressed Harding High freshmen and sophomores passed her. They were making their way across the student parking lot and into the gym where the Spring Fling was in full mode. She would have thought the "Over the Rainbow" theme was intentionally mocking her, but she knew it had been voted on weeks before her party that never was.

"Can I help you?" she asked some little freshmen gawkers. They just sneered at her and continued on inside.

She had figured it would be like this. It wasn't her choice to miss the entire week of school. The doctor said she was fine to go in. But her father had thought it would be best, under the circumstances. Gin knew better. She knew that every day absent was a missed opportunity to run damage control. But her father had put his foot down for once. She still remembered the look of disappointment on his face. To say nothing of the screaming her mother had done.

That was new too.

She had totally gotten away with the party, though. Her father didn't notice the balloons were condoms. And wasn't even suspicious when Rod showed up alone a few minutes later. But she couldn't hide everything from her parents. And when things came out last week, way after the aborted party, their relationship had changed.

Gin moved for the door, but stopped when she saw Jade Lawrence coming out and heading straight for her. Even though Jade was totally underdressed for the dance, she still looked stunning in her denim jeans and babydoll tee. Gin hated her just a little bit more for that.

"Hey Gin," Jade said. "That's a great dress."

"Thanks," Gin said. Even though her parents were upset with her, they had allowed her to pick up a really great red dress for the dance. She figured it was their way of letting her know everything would ultimately be all right. "You're a bit underdressed."

"Oh, no Spring Fling for me," Jade said. Then she seemed to think about something for a moment before adding, "My sister's getting married tomorrow."

"Really?" Gin asked. She didn't even know Jade had a sister. "That's . . . great."

"Well, not exactly 'great,'" Jade said cryptically. "But we're all getting used to the idea."

"Sorry you have to miss the dance, though," Gin said, not really meaning it.

"It's okay," Jade replied. "I went to my boyfriend's Prom last night."

Boyfriend?

Since when did Jade have a boyfriend? It wasn't often that Gin was shocked about anything. She was usually well tuned into the grapevine . . . but she had been a little out of the loop lately.

"How was it?" Gin asked.

Jade got this odd look on her face. "It was amazing. Absolutely perfect."

For some reason, Gin suspected that Jade wasn't talking about dancing.

"I didn't think that you'd be here tonight," Jade said.

"Well, it *is* the social event of the season," Gin replied sarcastically. "If I didn't show up, everyone would be talking."

Jade suddenly looked very uncomfortable.

"That was a joke," Gin said. "I know I'm already the main topic of conversation."

"Look, I know this is none of my business," Jade said, "but if you ever want to talk . . . or just hang out . . . whatever . . ."

"Thanks," Gin said. She wasn't entirely shocked. Jade was always looking for a new project. Gin just figured that she was it. This was, however, the longest conversation the two of them had ever had. Things must be really ugly inside for Jade to take an interest in her.

"Well, gotta go," Jade said. "My sister's probably a wreck right now."

"Wish her the best," Gin said. Not that Jade's sister knew who the hell Gin was.

"I will. Thanks," Jade said as she hurried off.

Gin took a deep breath and entered the gym wing.

The halls outside the gym were decorated with papier-mâché flowers and a yellow brick road leading down to the dance. It looked absolutely ridiculous. But Gin wasn't focused on the decorations. She was looking at the kids moving toward the gym, hoping to avoid certain people, while searching for one person in particular.

Rod was the first person she saw that she knew. He was with some random freshman girl who was hanging on to his arm like he was some big prize or something. Of course he was with a freshman. No sophomore girl would touch him after word got around how he treated Skye. It wasn't so much the cheating, but the whole thing with her best friend that pissed everyone off. Gin had actually heard the screaming fight between Rod and Skye in the lunchroom the day the truth finally came out.

Gin was shocked that it had taken a full week after the party.

She hadn't expected Rod to get a new girl that fast, but he was disease free, which probably helped.

"Hey, Gin," Steve Jacobs said angrily from behind her. "Thanks a *lot.*"

She turned to find him in a horribly tight suit jacket that looked like he had last worn it to his confirmation two years and a growth spurt ago.

"Excuse me?" Gin said.

"The gonorrhea," Steve said, way too loudly in the crowded hall. "Thanks for that."

Since Gin really didn't give a damn what Steve said to her, she didn't say anything. He was the one that had gone after her. Steve could have just as easily given it to her.

"Bitch!" he said, before storming off.

There were a few things that Gin felt badly about. Steve Jacobs was not one of them.

At last report, thirty-nine members of the sophomore class had gotten gonorrhea. Of that thirty-nine only two—or possibly three—were supposed to be at her party. And even though it never happened, somehow she was the one getting all the blame.

If only her parents hadn't taken her out of a week of school. It was going to be brutal facing everyone this way.

Gin continued to the gym and handed her ticket to the chaperones working the door. Before she could head inside, something caught her attention. There was a girl dressed as what looked like a Japanese anime character.

She wasn't sure, but under the heavy makeup it seemed like it was . . . but it couldn't be . . .

"Rose?"

Gin figured that it was Rose because Ash was clinging to her arm. Plus, who else would dress that way to a dance that wasn't costume-themed.

"Gin," Rose said in a surprisingly subdued voice. "Can you believe Mrs. Steiner won't let me in? She says I'm not in an appropriate outfit. And Principal Hogan refuses to come out to help."

"Are you supposed to be a Munchkin?" Gin asked, trying not to laugh.

"No," Rose said. "I'm just going for a different look."

"Well, you've certainly succeeded," Gin said.

"I think she looks hot," Ash said as he squeezed her tightly to him.

They were so unbearably cute together. But for the first time, Gin didn't want to barf around them. She must be mellowing. Or maybe they were just growing on her.

"So . . . how are you?" Rose asked.

"Pretty good, considering," Gin replied. "Guess you guys are happy you're only sleeping with each other, huh?"

"Actually, we're more content with the fact that we're not," Ash said abruptly.

Gin saw Rose's eyes go wider than her heavy makeup had prepared for. Once again, Gin was surprised at how this piece of news wasn't nearly as interesting as it should have been to her.

"So, what are you going to do about the dance?" Gin asked, changing the subject.

"Oh, I'm getting in there," Rose said. "If I have to get Jade to go after Hogan for me."

"Somehow, I think you'll be fine on your own," Gin said. She looked down the hall and saw the principal going out a side door. "Um . . . I think he's trying to escape."

"Thanks, Gin," Rose said as she hurried down the hall after him. "Don't think I don't see you, Mr. Hogan."

"There goes the girl I love," Ash said as he followed.

Gin smiled. It was a bit of a relief. She actually forgot about her own situation for a moment.

But now it was time to enter the party. And face the music.

Gin stepped inside the gym, hoping to be transported to another world. But there were just more papier-mâché flowers and rainbows made of balloons . . . *real* balloons, not condoms.

Oh look, there's patient zero now.

Gin had no proof that Hunter had been the one to start the spread of gonorrhea through the sophomore class, but she just had this feeling. Of course, he had been the one to sound the alarm, which made him some kind of hero, while Gin was relegated to town slut.

Hypocrites.

"Hunter," Gin said coldly. She was glad to see that he seemed to be alone. "Going solo?"

"Not at all," Hunter said. "My date's just over there getting us some punch."

She hated herself for thinking it, but he looked incredibly hot in his suit.

"Hey Gin," Perry said.

"Third-wheeling it?" she asked.

Perry just shrugged.

It was really pathetic how Perry followed Hunter around. Gin wanted to say something about it, but she didn't. Perry was the only one who called her during the past week, keeping her up-to-date on everything. It was kind of weird that the two of them were getting closer.

It was surprising the things they had in common.

"How you feeling?" Perry asked.

"Perfectly fine," Gin said. "The doctor said everything's running its course."

"Me too," Hunter added. "A clean bill of health. I just have to avoid sex for a little while and then I can get right back on the horse . . . so to speak."

Gin didn't feel that needed any comment. She wanted to ask Perry how he was doing, but she wasn't really sure that he had been one of the thirty-nine. Actually, that wasn't true at all. She was pretty sure that Perry *was* infected. In fact, she suspected that Perry had been the first one diagnosed and made Hunter send an e-mail chain to alert everyone about the outbreak. But Perry would never let anyone at school know that.

He was too good at keeping secrets.

"So . . . maybe we can hook up sometime soon," Hunter said.

Gin considered it for a moment.

"You know," Hunter continued. "I figure you owed me one, for catching it in time."

"Such a tempting offer," Gin said. "But I think I'm going to pass."

Gin turned and walked away before he could respond. She did this mainly because she didn't trust herself not to change her mind.

The doctor had caught the infection early enough that she would be totally in the clear pretty soon. But Gin knew she owed that more to Perry than Hunter. Besides, what kind of a lowlife would expect to be repaid with sexual favors simply for informing you that he had given you an STD?

Hunter was unbelievable. She didn't know why she hadn't seen it sooner. Well, she *had* seen it before. She'd just ignored it.

It took Gin a couple of minutes to work her way through the whispering crowd. Of course, since the music was so loud, the whispers were fairly audible. She finally found Sandy on the edge of the dance floor along with Skye and Vi.

"Hi," Gin said.

Sandy didn't even turn to face her.

Even though the music was louder on the dance floor, Gin was pretty sure Sandy could hear her.

"Sandy!" Gin shouted, practically in her ear.

This time, Sandy was forced to turn. Unfortunately, Skye and Vi had turned to face her as well.

"Oh, hi," Sandy said as she continued dancing.

"Didn't expect to see you here," Skye interrupted.

"You either," Gin replied. "I thought you were grounded for life."

"Mom was more lenient, once I tested negative," Skye said. "And when she found out I was never going to see Rod again."

"And you told her you weren't even thinking of going to the dance with a boy," Vi added.

"Well, there's that," Skye agreed.

Gin was surprised to see them getting along so well. It was pretty clear that Skye hadn't believed Vi when she first mentioned that Rod had hit on her. The two of them didn't even speak for a week. But then came the infamous lunch-room confrontation and all apparently was healed between them.

It was even more surprising to see them welcoming Sandy into their little clique.

"I've been trying to call you," Gin said.

"Oh," Sandy said. "I didn't know." There was something in the way that she said it that was not convincing in the least.

Sandy's parents had always said that she was busy whenever Gin called in the past week. Gin figured they didn't want her talking to their daughter. It *was* odd that Sandy hadn't called her on her own since finding out that Gin was sick.

"Mind if I join the group?" Gin asked.

"Do you think you should?" Sandy asked. "Should you really be exerting yourself like that?"

Gin knew Sandy. She was the kind of girl that would have immediately looked up the symptoms and cure for gonorrhea on WebMD the moment she heard it was spreading. Of course it was fine for Gin to be dancing.

"Can we talk?" Gin asked.

"Right now?" Sandy asked. "I love this song."

Gin found that *really* hard to believe. The DJ was playing some classic Nine Inch Nails.

"Well, can we get together tomorrow?" Gin persisted.

Sandy broke away from her new friends for the moment. Gin figured this couldn't possibly be good.

"Look, Gin," Sandy said. "My parents don't want me hanging out with you anymore. I mean, at least for a while. I'm sure they'll calm down soon. It's just—"

"No. I get it," Gin said. And she did. What she didn't get was the fact that Sandy didn't seem to be nearly as upset about what happened to Gin as she should be.

"Maybe in a couple weeks," Sandy said. Gin could even hear the hollowness of the promise over the music.

"Sure," Gin said. There was nothing more to say, so she walked away from the dance floor and out of the gym entirely.

This was a mistake.

Gin walked through more whispers out in the hall and straight out of the building. As soon as she was outside, she pulled a cigarette from her purse and put it between her Harlot lips.

"I didn't know you had taken up smoking," Ms. Barrett said, just as Gin was lighting up.

"Didn't you hear? Apparently I have an oral fixation."

"Funny," Ms. Barrett said, though neither of them was laughing.

"Nice dress," Ms. Barrett said. "Very Scarlett O'Hara."

"I was going for that," Gin said, looking down at the dress that matched her lips. "I thought it would be fitting. I would have sewn a letter on it, but that would be over the top, don't you think?"

"Undoubtedly."

"So, I heard you quit," Gin said as she took a puff.

"Word travels fast around here," Ms. Barrett said.

"Rumor has it you had some kind of breakdown."

"I heard that one too," Ms. Barrett said. "I prefer it to the rumor that I was pregnant with Hunter's baby. I mean, really." She paused to roll her eyes at the thought of that.

"It had more to do with the hypocrisy of being admonished—twice—for teaching safer sex right before an outbreak of gonorrhea," Ms. Barrett admitted. "Ultimately I think I made the right decision."

"Glad I could help," Gin said.

"Well at least you've kept your sense of humor."

"It's about all I've got, at the moment," Gin said. "Sandy won't even speak to me."

"Give her time," Ms. Barrett said. "She'll come around."

"And if she doesn't?"

"You could always move to another state."

"Big help," Gin said, but she couldn't help smiling.

"I know how resilient you are, Gin," Ms. Barrett said. "Outcast today . . . class president tomorrow. Just take it one day at a time."

"Thanks for the cliché."

"No problem," Ms. Barrett said as she grabbed the cigarette from Gin's mouth and stomped it out on the ground. "Now I've got to get back in there before anything unseemly happens. You never know what these kids will get up to these days."

"You really don't," Gin agreed.

She watched as the teacher went back into the building. She was really going to miss Ms. Barrett.

Gin was about to start the walk home when she saw an interesting foursome coming her way. Brick and Allison along with Rusty and that new girl.

"Well, isn't this cute?" Gin said as they approached.

Rusty looked rather tense. Brick and Allison looked uncomfortable. The new girl looked . . . well, like she could give Jade a run for Most Popular.

"I didn't know you guys were together," Gin said to Brick.

"We just started," Allison replied.

"Well, congratulations," Gin said. She meant it too. She didn't know Brick had it in him. The best way to confront the jokes about his virginity was to take them head-on. And the best way to do that was to date the head of the Celibacy Club.

"Got a minute?" she asked Rusty.

His eyes filled with horror. "Uh . . . sure. Why don't you guys wait for me inside?"

"That's okay," the new girl said. "We don't mind."

"Well, I do," Brick said. "It's getting cold out here. Let's go." Since he already had Allison on his right arm, he held out his left for the new girl. Gin watched as she took his arm. Gin gave him extra points for the fact that it was obvious he was just covering for Rusty so he could talk to Gin alone.

"You know she's out of your league," Gin said once they were out of earshot.

"You had your chance," Rusty said. "I guess it's a good thing we only did it the one time."

"You're clean?"

"Yeah," he said. "But I still needed to go on antibiotics, just in case. That was a fun conversation with my parents."

This time Gin felt like she should apologize, but she wasn't really sure what she was apologizing for. She hadn't known she was infected when they hooked up. At least he wasn't pissed at her.

"Can I give you some advice?" Gin asked, but didn't wait for an answer. "The new girl—she really is out of your league."

"She has a name, you know," Rusty said. "And it's really none of your business."

"True," Gin said. "But when has that stopped me before?"

Rusty shook his head, but couldn't help smiling.

"What kind of girl transfers into a school with only a month left in the year, anyway?"

"Her dad's job takes her all over the place," he explained. "It's not the first time."

"And you were probably the first guy at school to talk to her," Gin said.

"So what?"

"So she's only interested in you because of that," Gin explained. "She doesn't really like you."

"Because she out of my league?"

"Exactly."

"And just out of curiosity," Rusty said, looking pissed, "are *you* in my league?"

"Oh God, no." Gin laughed. "I'm out of your league too."

"Then what the—"

"Sandy," Gin said. "Sandy is in your league. In fact, she's perfect for you."

"Really?" Rusty said, looking slightly more intrigued than annoyed. "I think Sandy's a little . . . inexperienced."

"Not for you," Gin said. "At any rate . . . once the new girl dumps you, give Sandy a call."

"If you know so much about who should be going with who, then why didn't you say anything before?" Rusty asked. "Sandy's supposed to be your best friend. Why is this the first time you're bringing it up?"

Gin licked her lips. Not only was Harlot a bad color, but the cheap Taboo Teen brand was making her lips dry.

"Why do you think I invited you to my party in the first place?"

Printed in the United States
92442LV00003B/118-450/A